FAR OUT FABLES

STONE ARCH BOOKS

a capstone imprint

INTRODUCING...

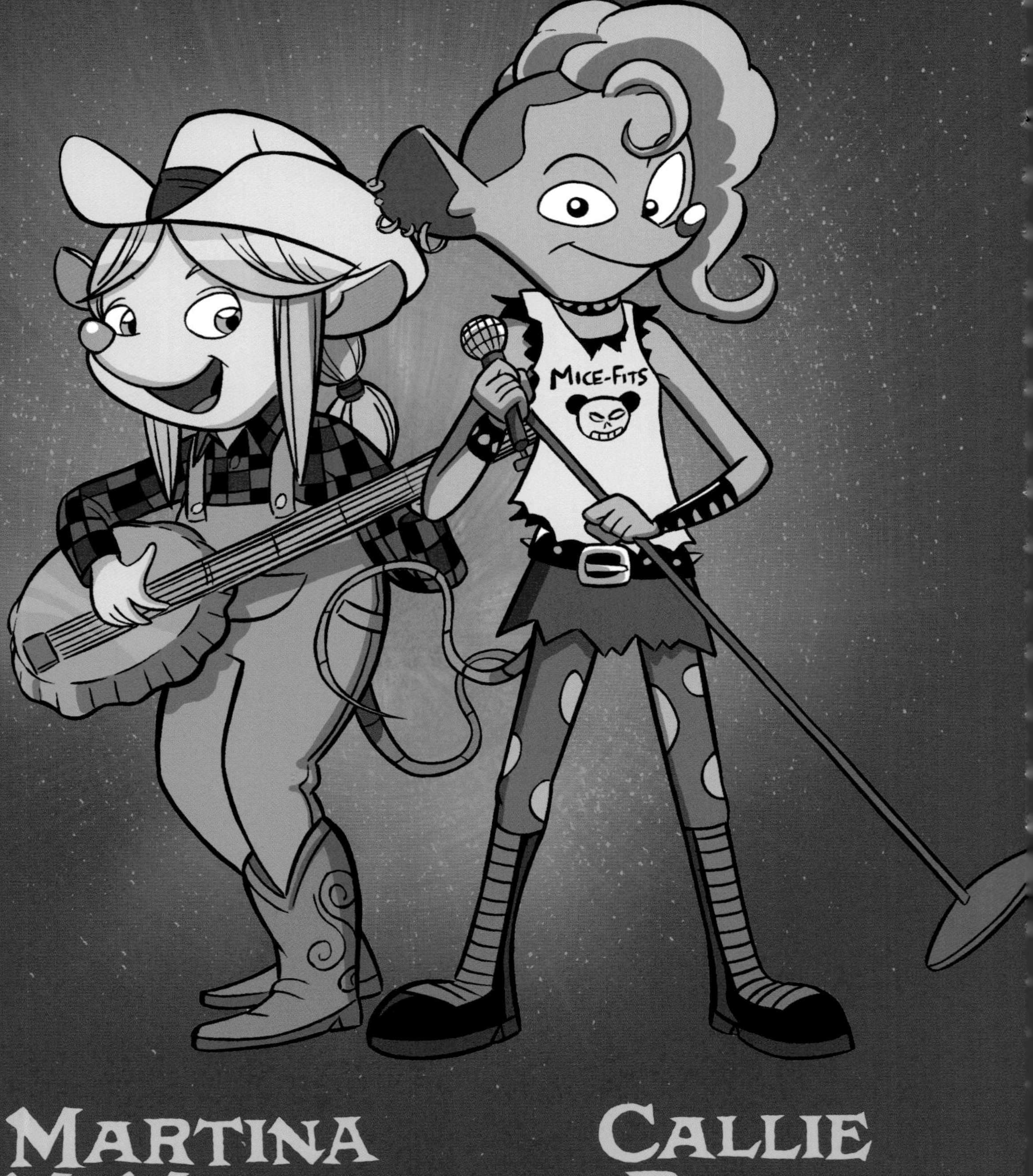
MICE-FITS

MARTINA McMOUSE

CALLIE RAAT

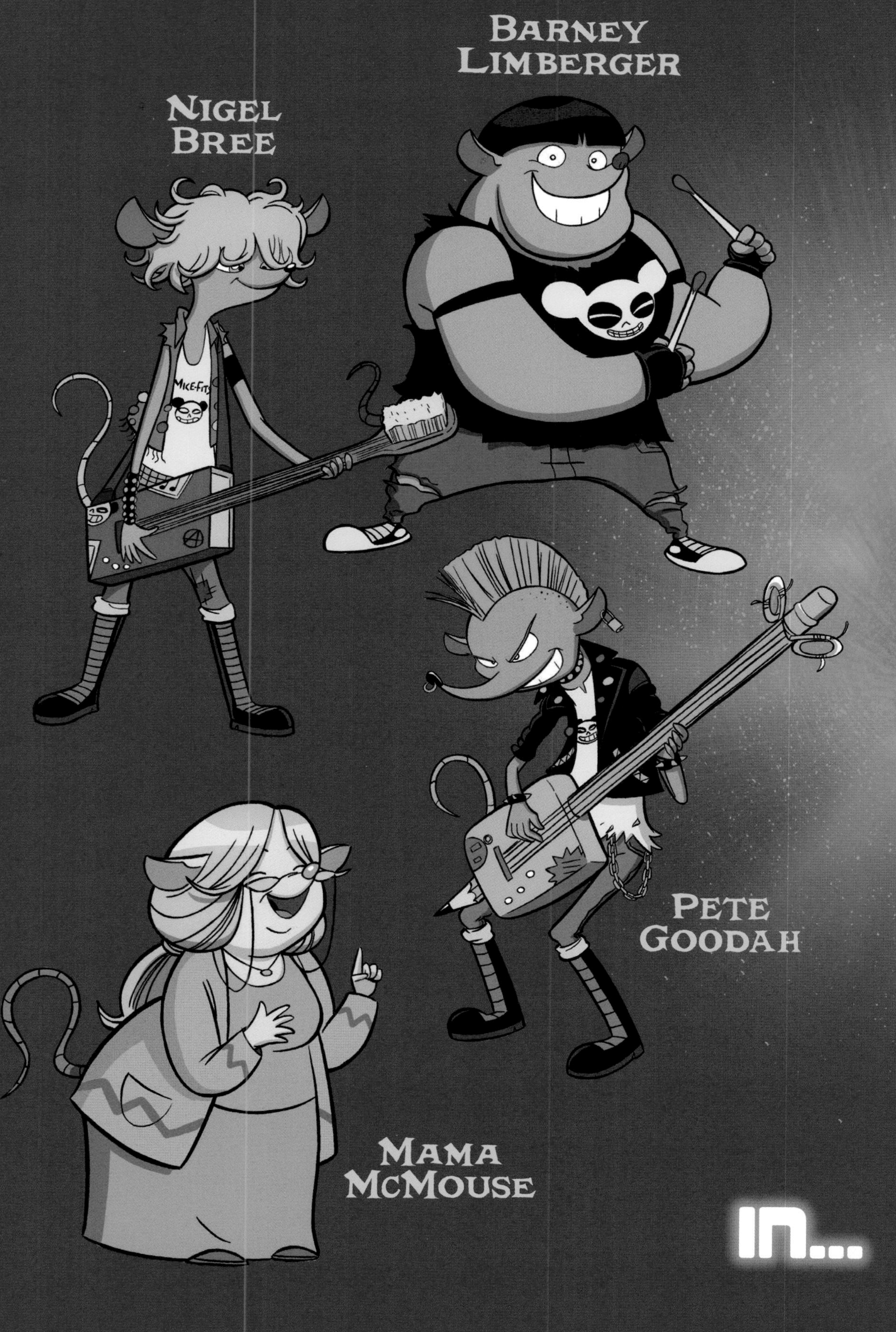

BARNEY LIMBERGER
NIGEL BREE
MICE-FITS
PETE GOODAH
MAMA McMOUSE
IN...

Far Out Fables is published by
Stone Arch Books,
an imprint of Capstone.
1710 Roe Crest Drive
North Mankato, Minnesota 56003
www.capstonepub.com

Cataloging-in-Publication Data is
available at the Library of Congress
website.

ISBN: 978-1-5158-8221-3 (hardcover)
ISBN: 978-1-5158-8330-2 (paperback)
ISBN: 978-1-5158-9218-2 (eBook PDF)

Summary: Callie and Martina are two
mice with almost nothing in common.
Callie is a punk rock star in the big
city who could use a little peace
and quiet. Martina is a singing farm
mouse with dreams of making it in
the big city. When they both show
up at the Battle of the Bands, Callie
and Martina get a taste of what
the other has to offer. But is living
another mouse's life really all it's
cracked up to be?

Designed by Hilary Wacholz
Edited by Mandy Robbins
Lettered by Jaymes Reed

Printed and bound in the United States of America. PO3837

FAR OUT FABLES

PUNK ROCK MOUSE
AND COUNTRY MOUSE

A GRAPHIC NOVEL

BY **BRANDON TERRELL**
ILLUSTRATED BY **ALEX LOPEZ**

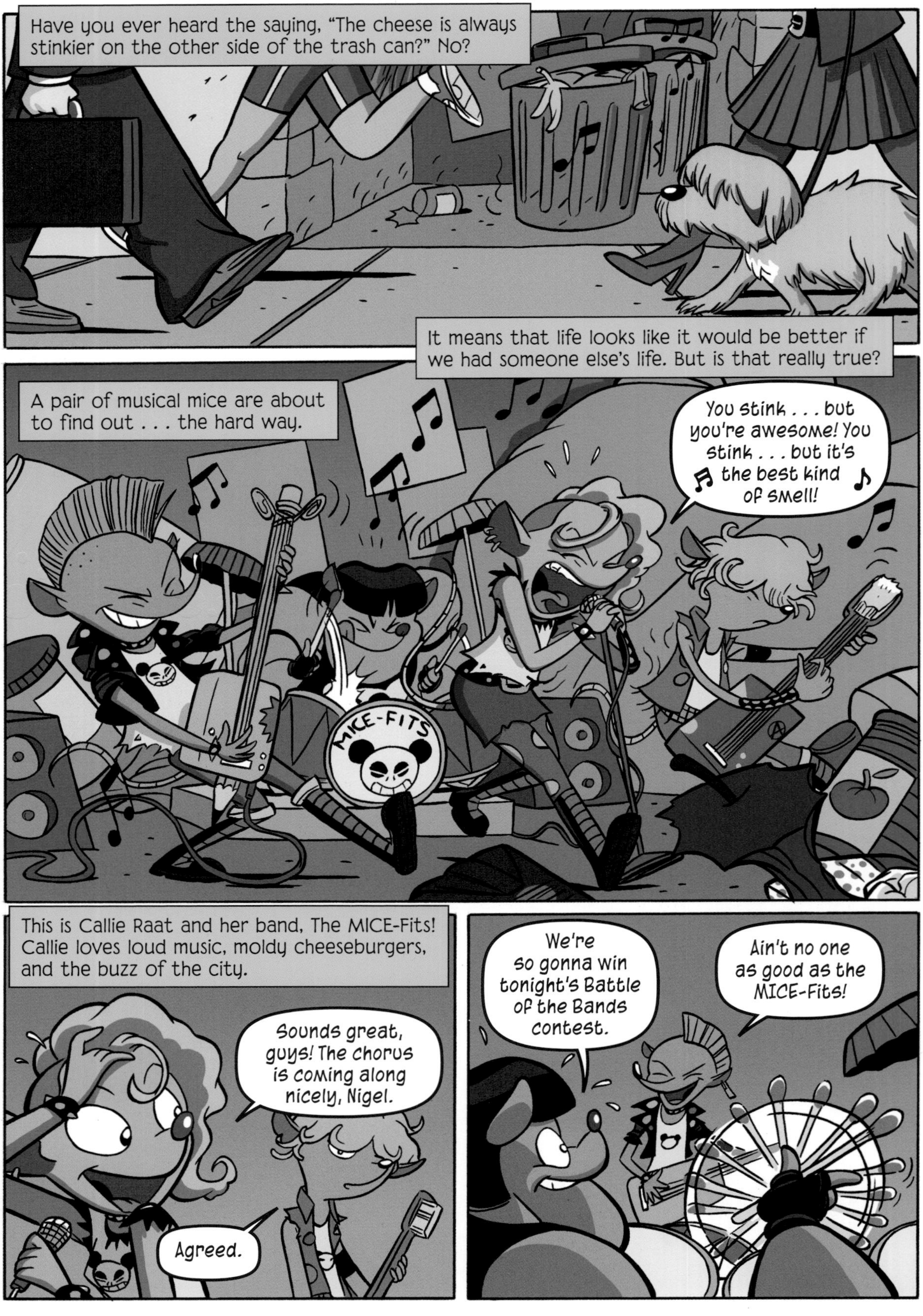
Have you ever heard the saying, "The cheese is always stinkier on the other side of the trash can?" No?
It means that life looks like it would be better if we had someone else's life. But is that really true?
A pair of musical mice are about to find out . . . the hard way.
You stink . . . but you're awesome! You stink . . . but it's the best kind of smell!
MICE-FITS
This is Callie Raat and her band, The MICE-Fits! Callie loves loud music, moldy cheeseburgers, and the buzz of the city.
Sounds great, guys! The chorus is coming along nicely, Nigel.
Agreed.
We're so gonna win tonight's Battle of the Bands contest.
Ain't no one as good as the MICE-Fits!

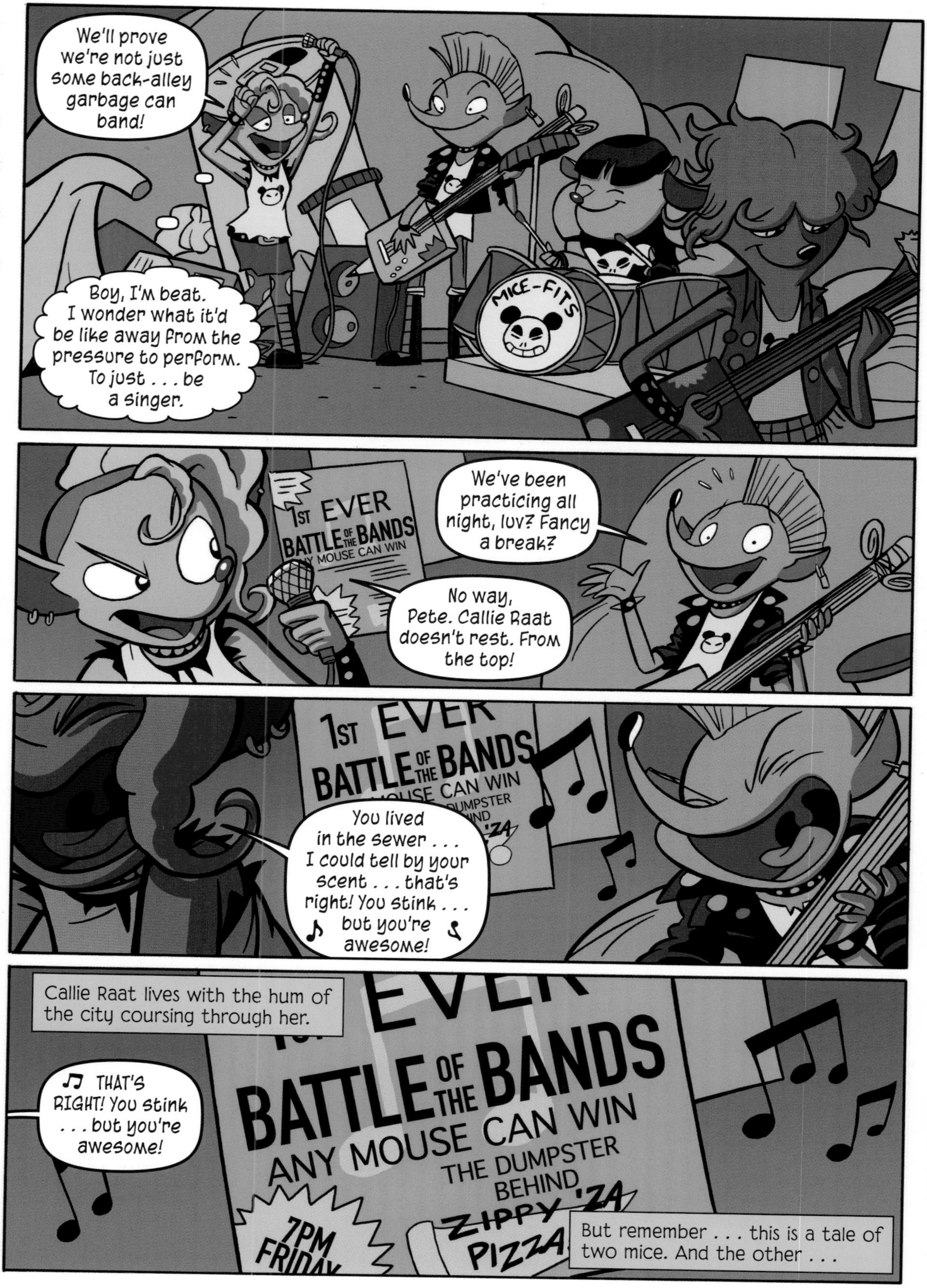
We'll prove we're not just some back-alley garbage can band!
Boy, I'm beat. I wonder what it'd be like away from the pressure to perform. To just . . . be a singer.
MICE-FITS
1ST EVER BATTLE OF THE BANDS ANY MOUSE CAN WIN
We've been practicing all night, luv? Fancy a break?
No way, Pete. Callie Raat doesn't rest. From the top!
1ST EVER BATTLE OF THE BANDS
You lived in the sewer . . . I could tell by your scent . . . that's right! You stink . . . but you're awesome!
Callie Raat lives with the hum of the city coursing through her.
THAT'S RIGHT! You stink . . . but you're awesome!
EVER BATTLE OF THE BANDS ANY MOUSE CAN WIN THE DUMPSTER BEHIND ZIPPY 'ZA PIZZA
7PM FRIDAY
But remember . . . this is a tale of two mice. And the other . . .

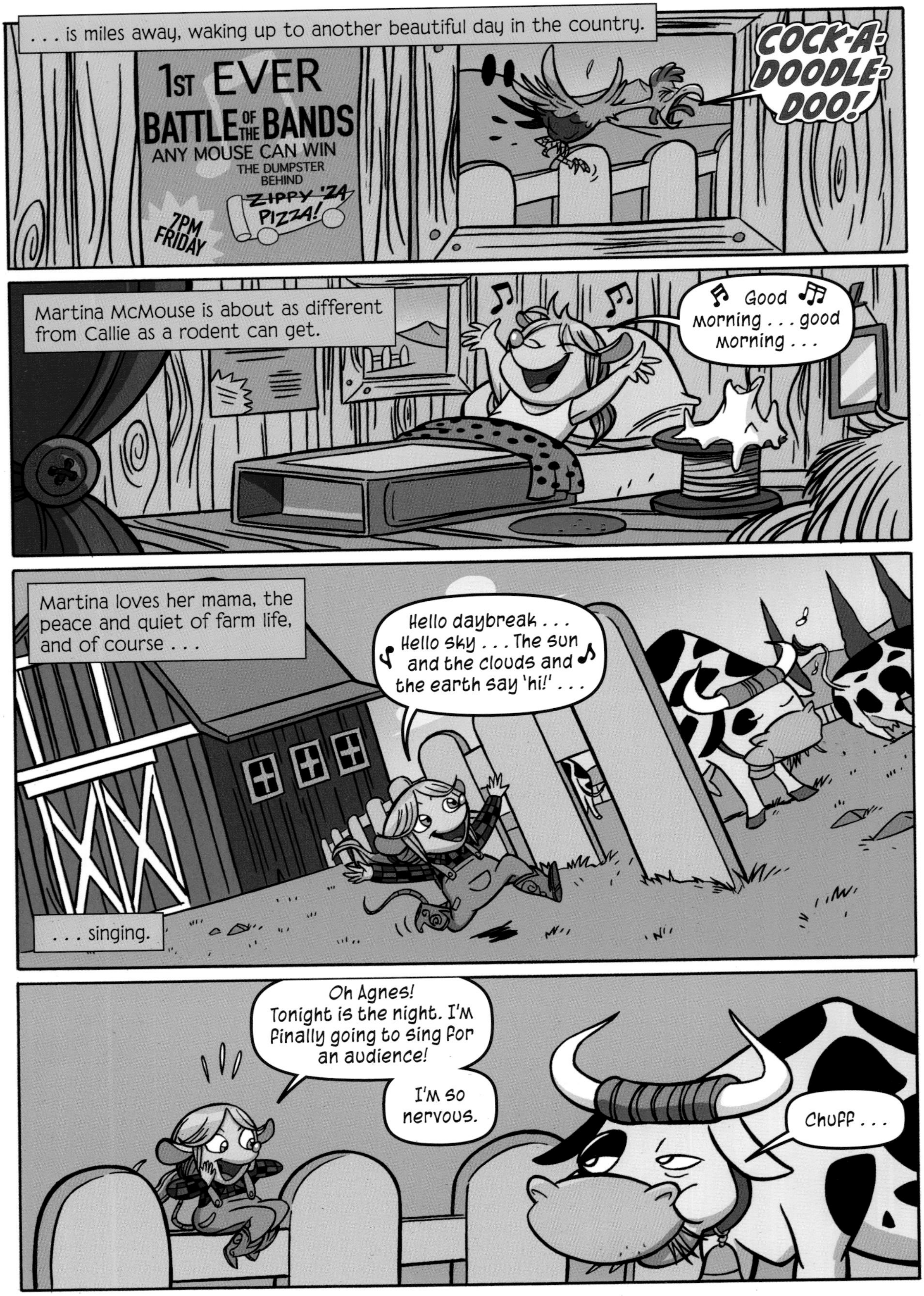
. . . is miles away, waking up to another beautiful day in the country.
1ST EVER BATTLE OF THE BANDS
ANY MOUSE CAN WIN
THE DUMPSTER BEHIND
ZIPPY 'ZA PIZZA!
7PM FRIDAY
COCK-A-DOODLE-DOO!
Martina McMouse is about as different from Callie as a rodent can get.
Good morning . . . good morning . . .
Martina loves her mama, the peace and quiet of farm life, and of course . . .
Hello daybreak . . . Hello sky . . . The sun and the clouds and the earth say 'hi!' . . .
. . . singing.
Oh Agnes! Tonight is the night. I'M finally going to sing for an audience!
I'M so nervous.
Chuff . . .

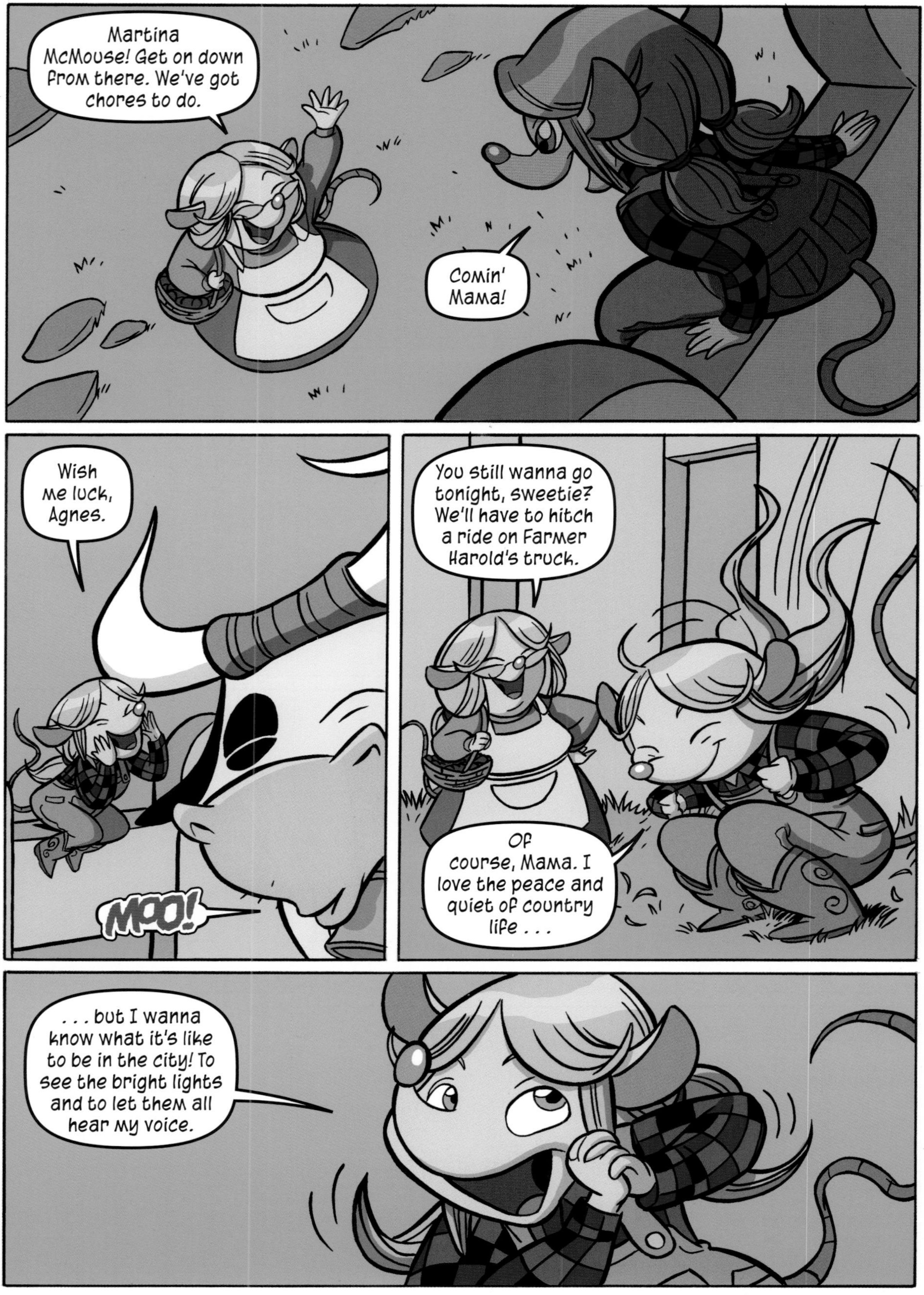
Martina McMouse! Get on down from there. We've got chores to do.
Comin' Mama!
Wish me luck, Agnes.
MOO!
You still wanna go tonight, sweetie? We'll have to hitch a ride on Farmer Harold's truck.
Of course, Mama. I love the peace and quiet of country life . . .
. . . but I wanna know what it's like to be in the city! To see the bright lights and to let them all hear my voice.

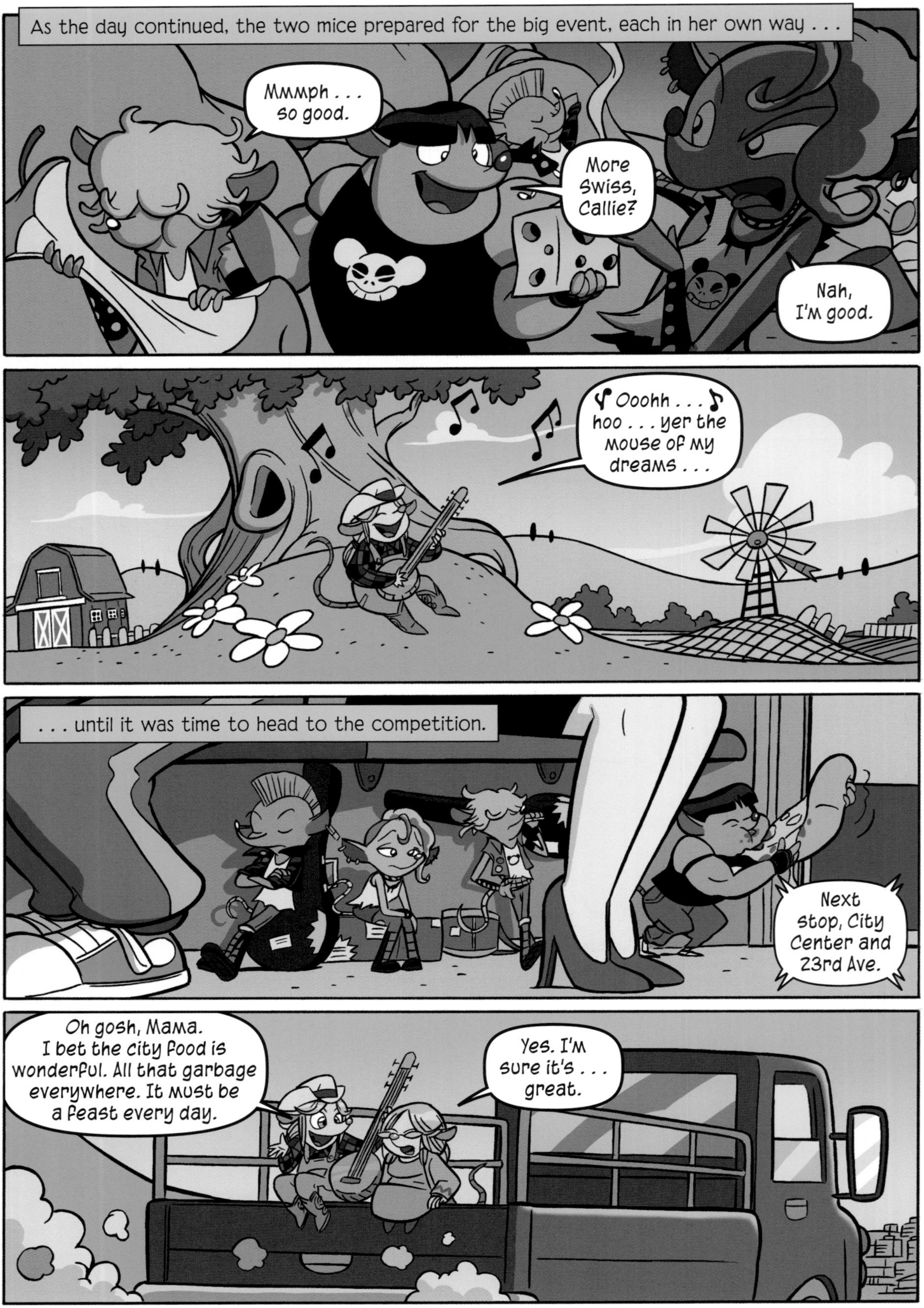

As the day continued, the two mice prepared for the big event, each in her own way . . .
Mmmph . . . so good.
More Swiss, Callie?
Nah, I'm good.
Ooohh . . . hoo . . . yer the mouse of my dreams . . .
. . . until it was time to head to the competition.
Next stop, City Center and 23rd Ave.
Oh gosh, Mama. I bet the city food is wonderful. All that garbage everywhere. It must be a feast every day.
Yes. I'm sure it's . . . great.

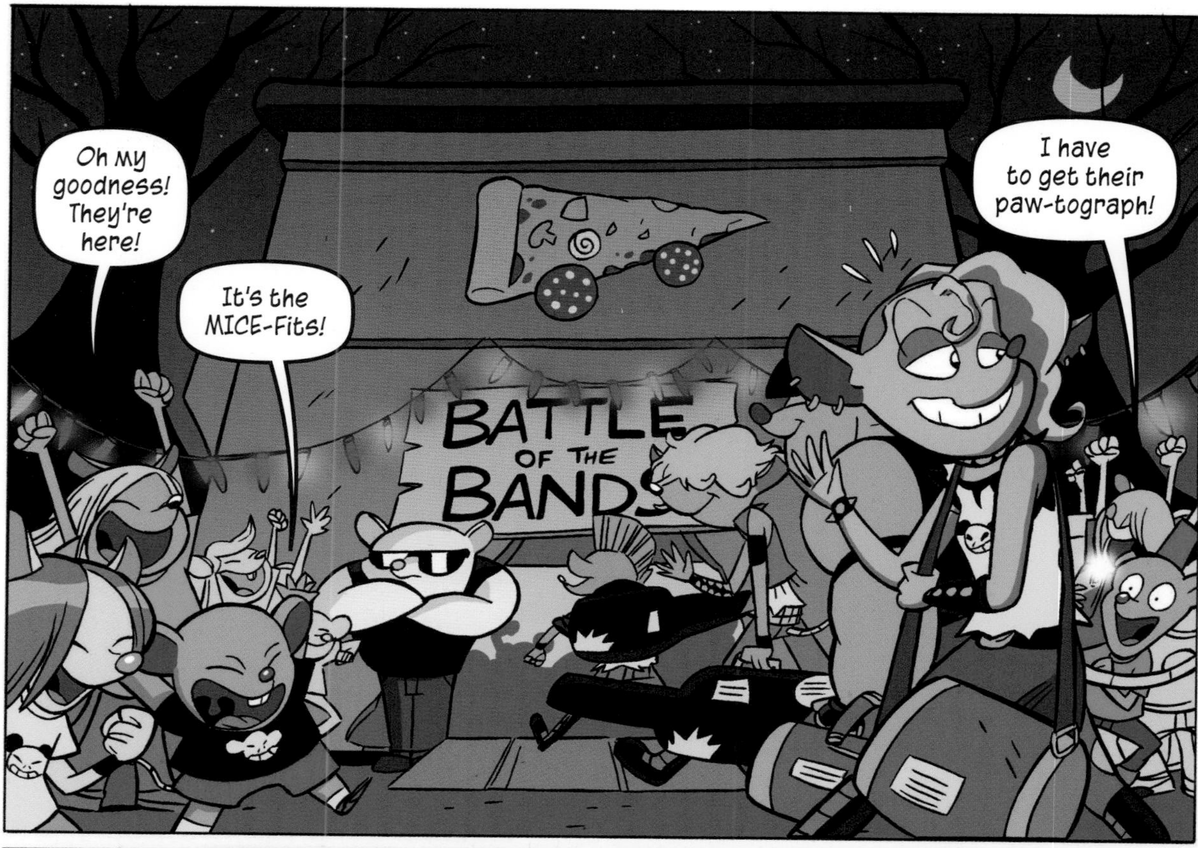
Oh my goodness! They're here!
It's the MICE-Fits!
I have to get their paw-tograph!
BATTLE OF THE BANDS

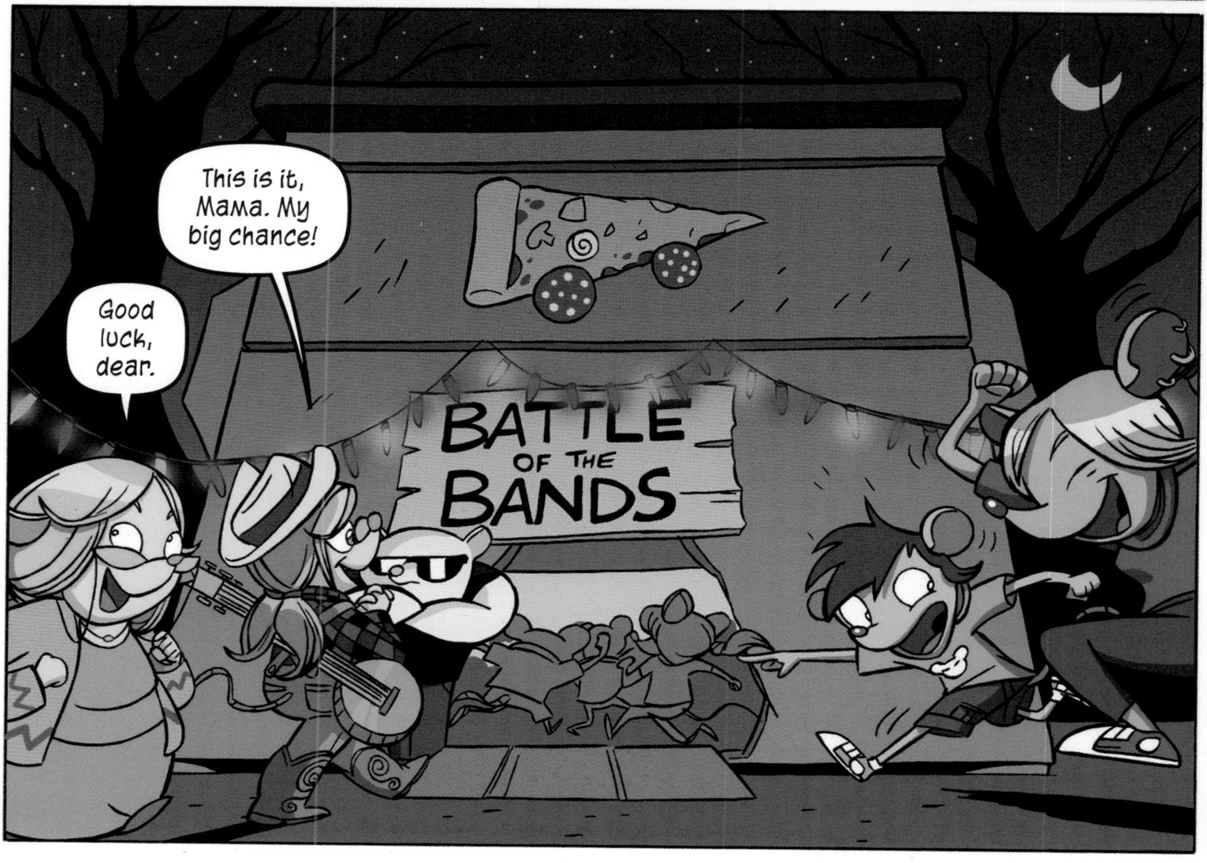
This is it, Mama. My big chance!
Good luck, dear.
BATTLE OF THE BANDS

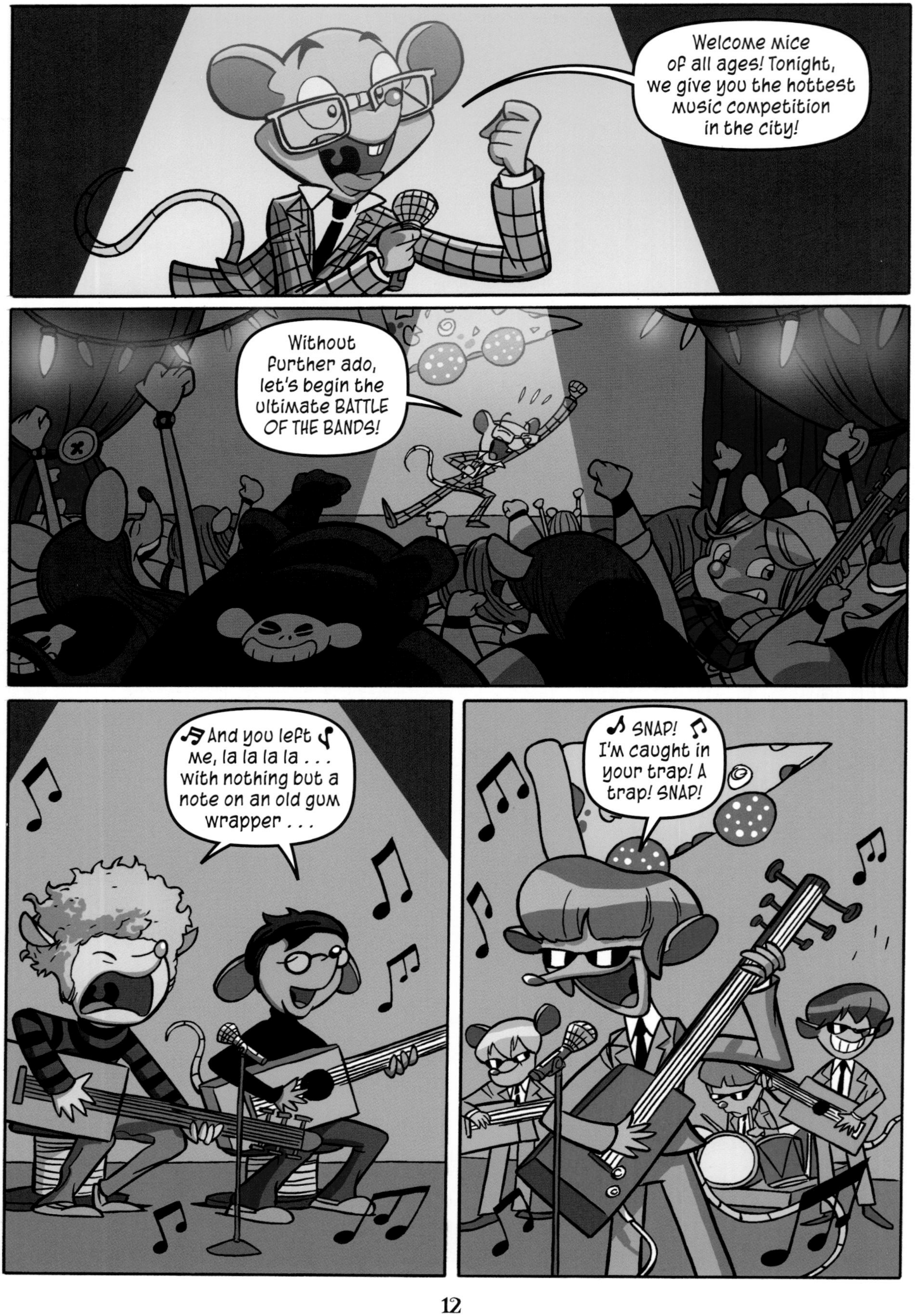
Welcome mice of all ages! Tonight, we give you the hottest music competition in the city!
Without further ado, let's begin the ultimate BATTLE OF THE BANDS!
And you left me, la la la la . . . with nothing but a note on an old gum wrapper . . .
SNAP! I'm caught in your trap! A trap! SNAP!

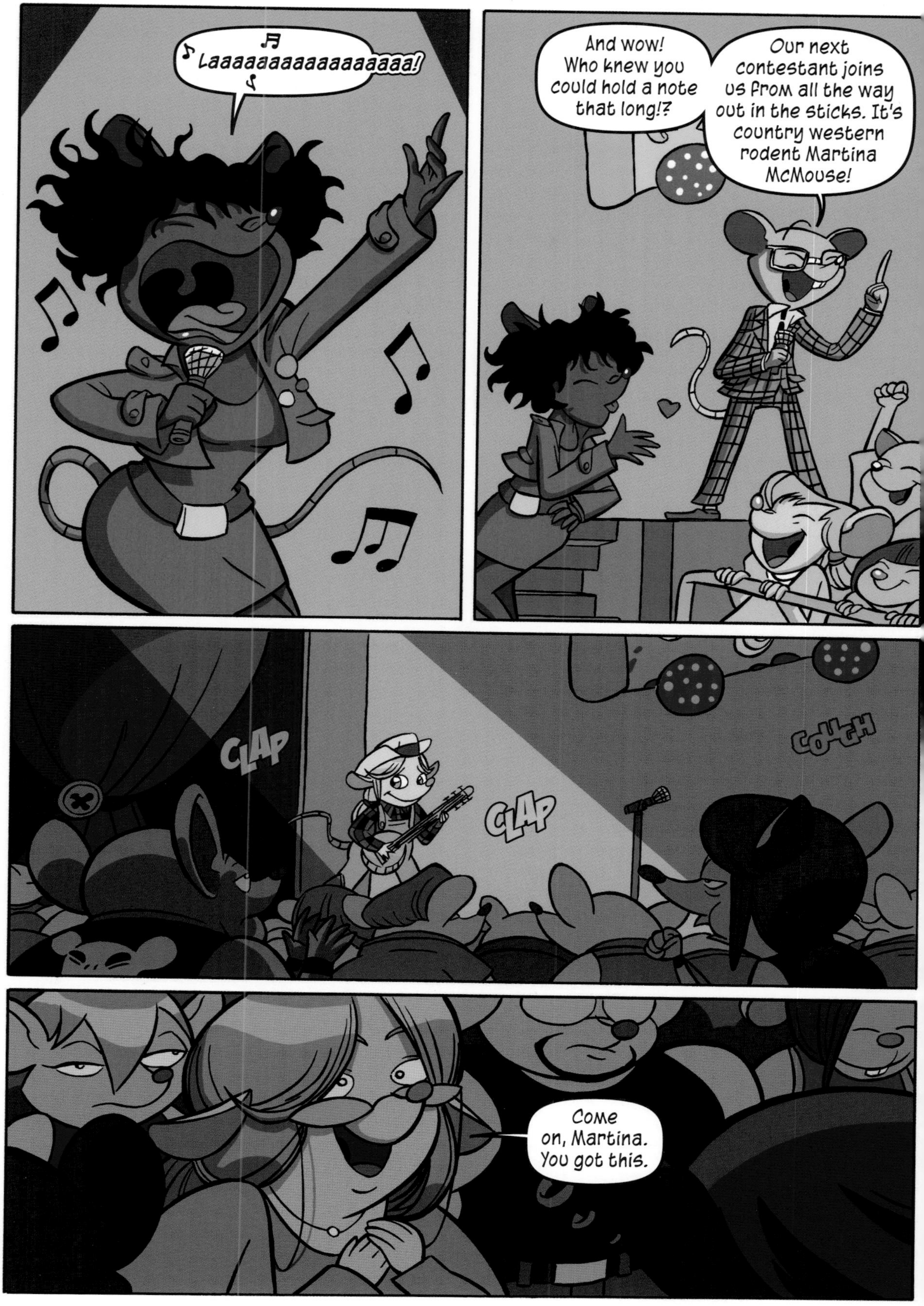
Laaaaaaaaaaaaaaaa!
And wow! Who knew you could hold a note that long!?
Our next contestant joins us from all the way out in the sticks. It's country western rodent Martina McMouse!
CLAP
CLAP
COUGH
Come on, Martina. You got this.

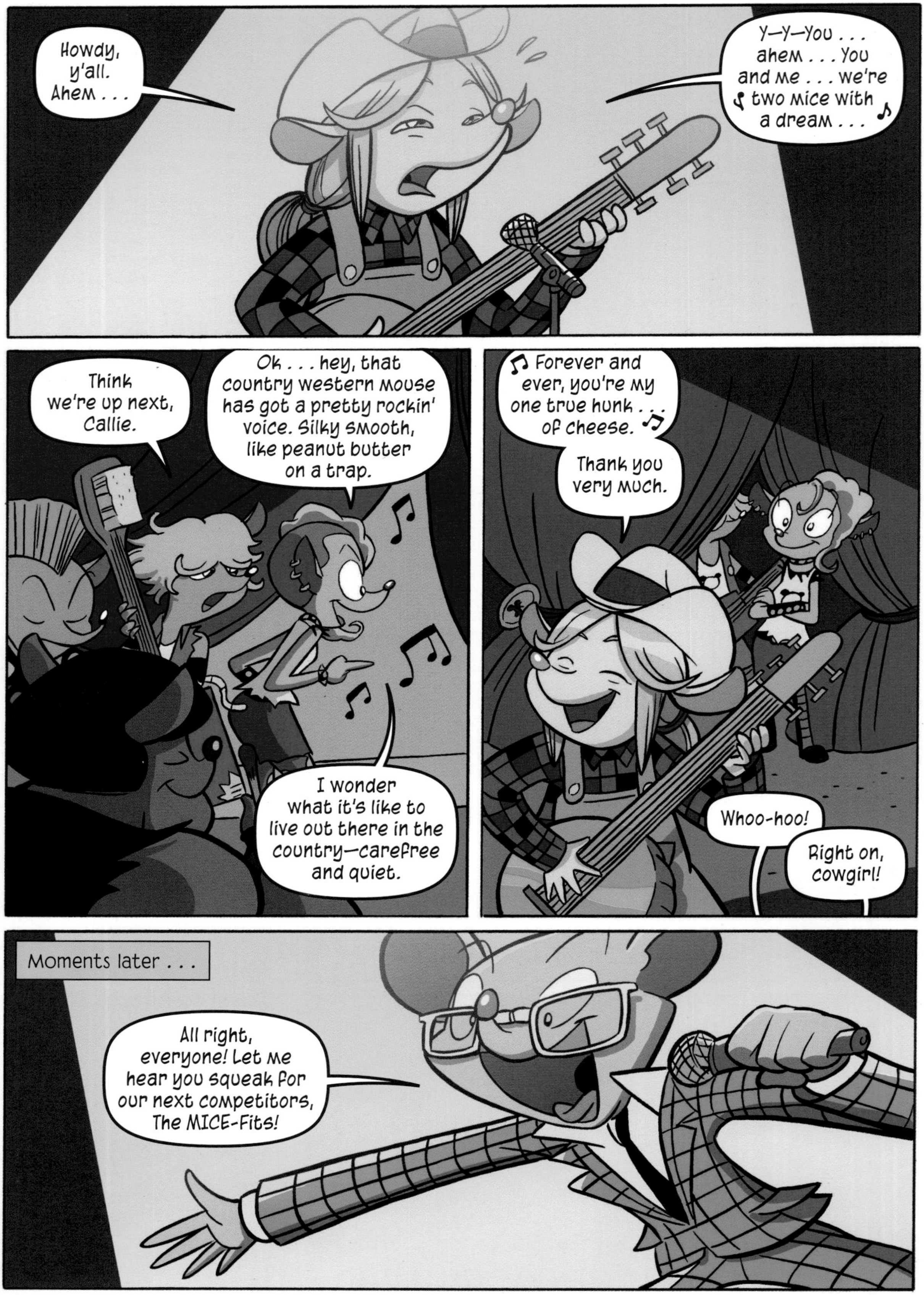
Howdy, y'all. Ahem . . .
Y—Y—You . . . ahem . . . You and me . . . we're two mice with a dream . . .
Think we're up next, Callie.
Ok . . . hey, that country western mouse has got a pretty rockin' voice. Silky smooth, like peanut butter on a trap.
I wonder what it's like to live out there in the country—carefree and quiet.
Forever and ever, you're my one true hunk . . . of cheese.
Thank you very much.
Whoo-hoo!
Right on, cowgirl!
Moments later . . .
All right, everyone! Let me hear you squeak for our next competitors, The MICE-Fits!

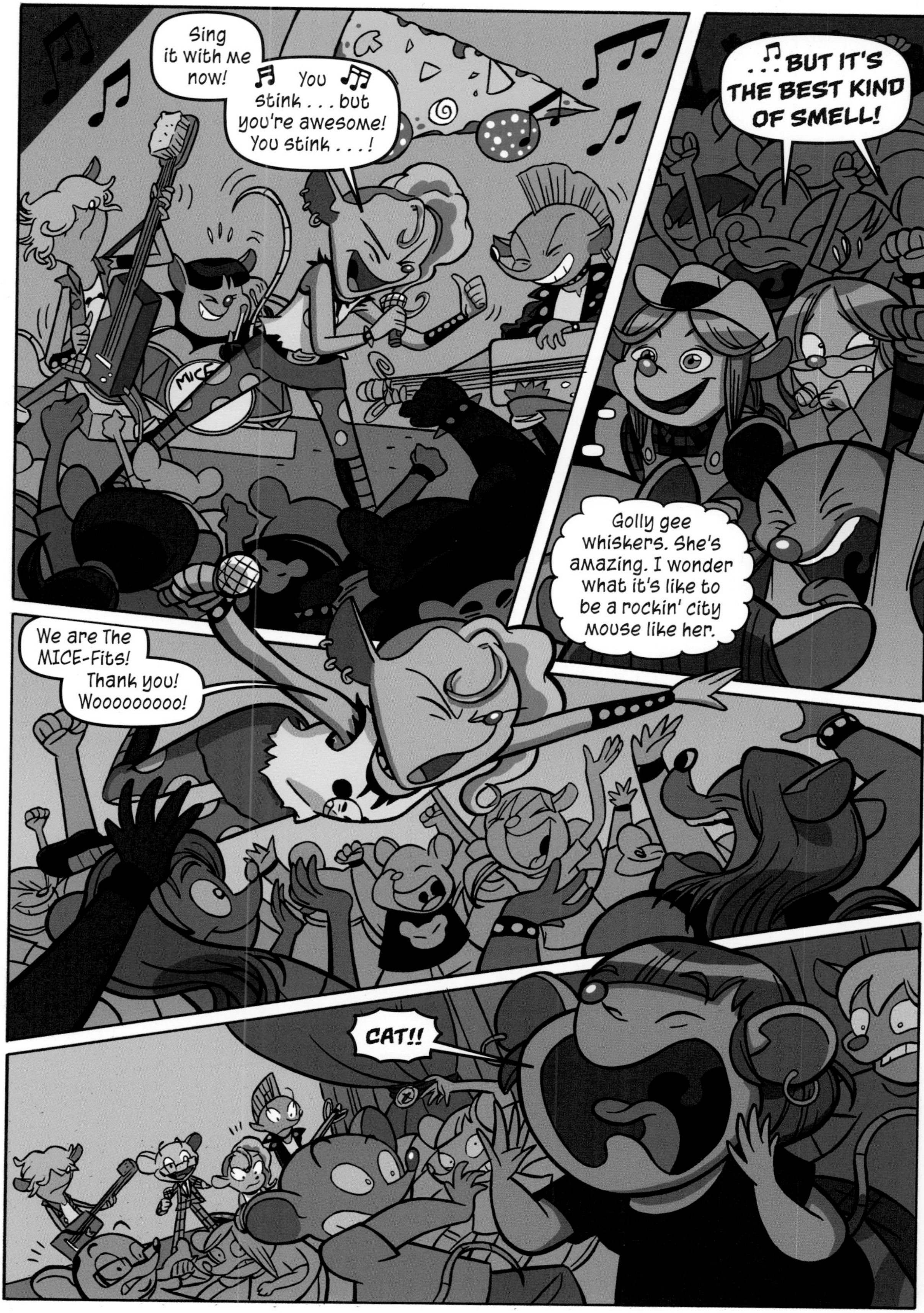
Sing it with me now!
♬ You ♬ stink . . . but you're awesome! You stink . . . !
. . .♫ BUT IT'S THE BEST KIND OF SMELL!
Golly gee whiskers. She's amazing. I wonder what it's like to be a rockin' city mouse like her.
We are the MICE-Fits! Thank you! Woooooooooo!
CAT!!

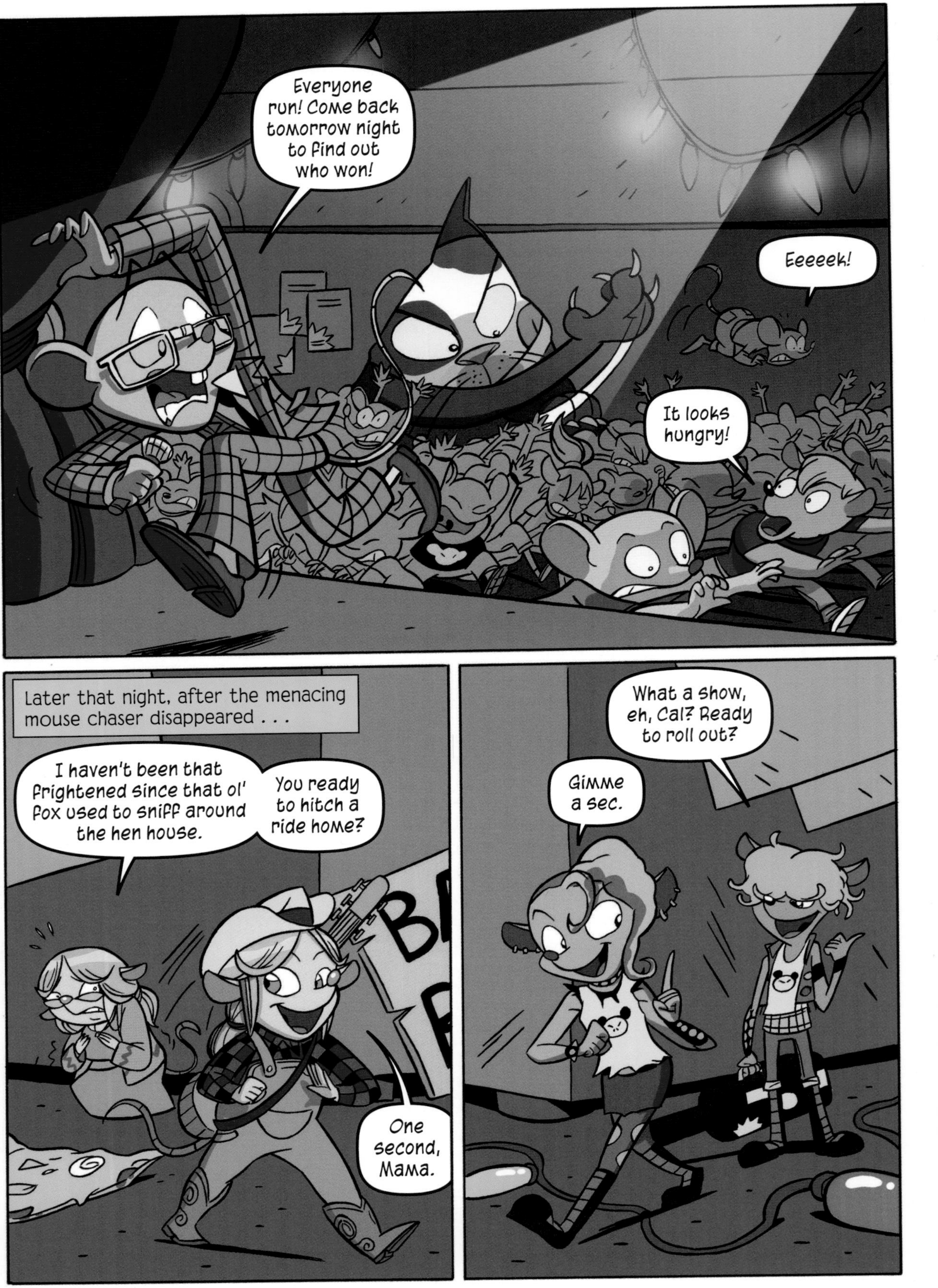
Everyone run! Come back tomorrow night to find out who won!
Eeeeek!
It looks hungry!
Later that night, after the menacing mouse chaser disappeared . . .
I haven't been that frightened since that ol' fox used to sniff around the hen house.
You ready to hitch a ride home?
One second, Mama.
What a show, eh, Cal? Ready to roll out?
Gimme a sec.

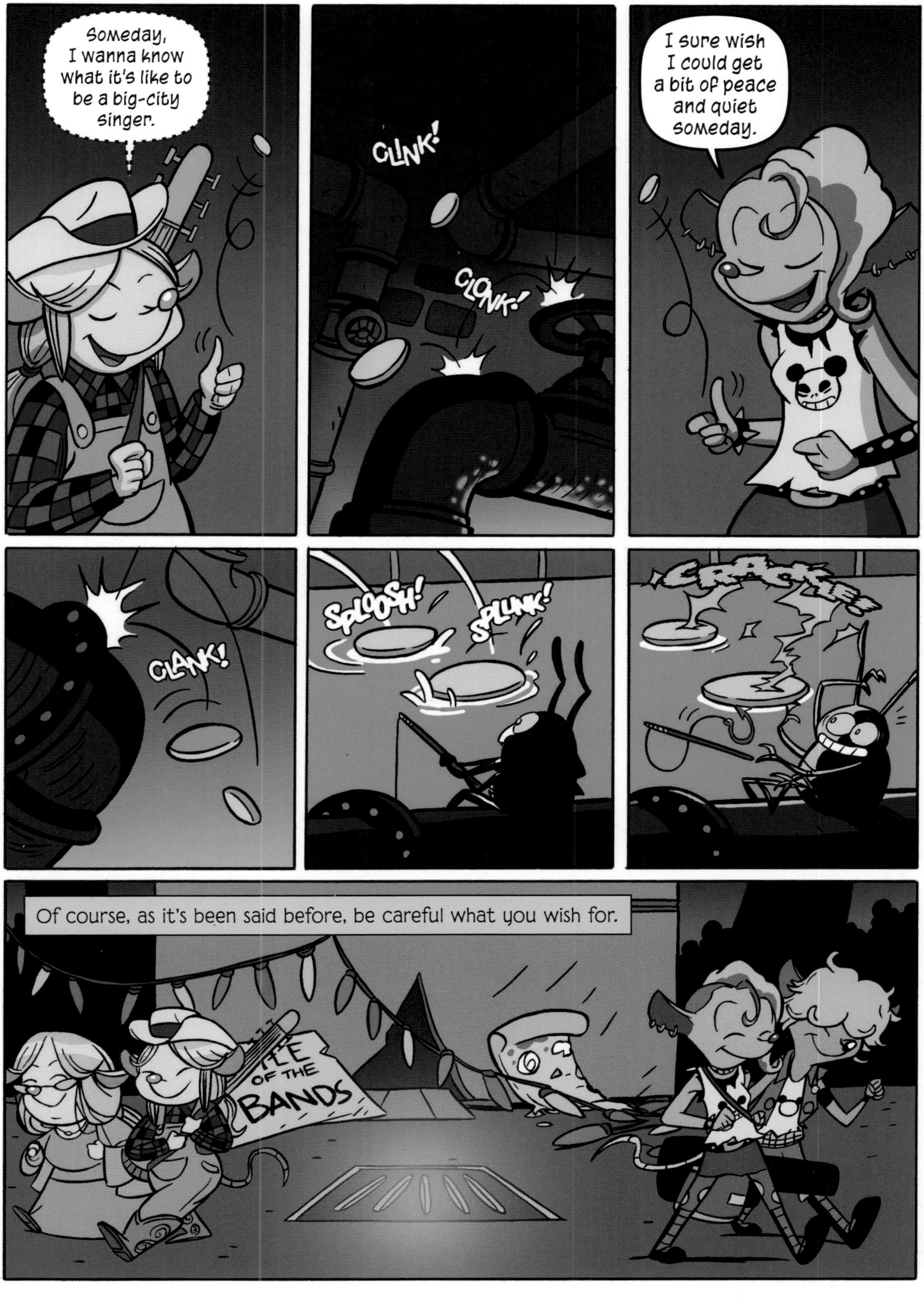
Someday, I wanna know what it's like to be a big-city singer.
CLINK!
CLONK!
I sure wish I could get a bit of peace and quiet someday.
CLANK!
SPLOOSH!
SPLUNK!
CRACKLE!
Of course, as it's been said before, be careful what you wish for.
OF THE BANDS

The following morning . . .

COCK-A-DOODLE-DOO!

snort . . . cough . . . What was that? Oooh, morning already.

Nigel? What was that noise?

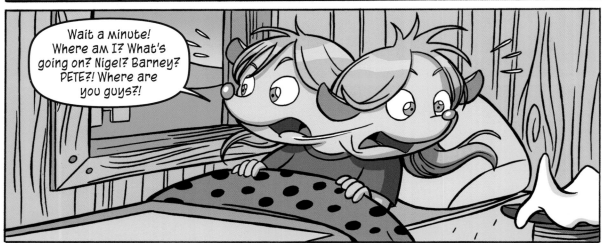

Wait a minute! Where am I? What's going on? Nigel? Barney? PETE?! Where are you guys?!

No way . . . No no no . . . I'm the country singer from the show!

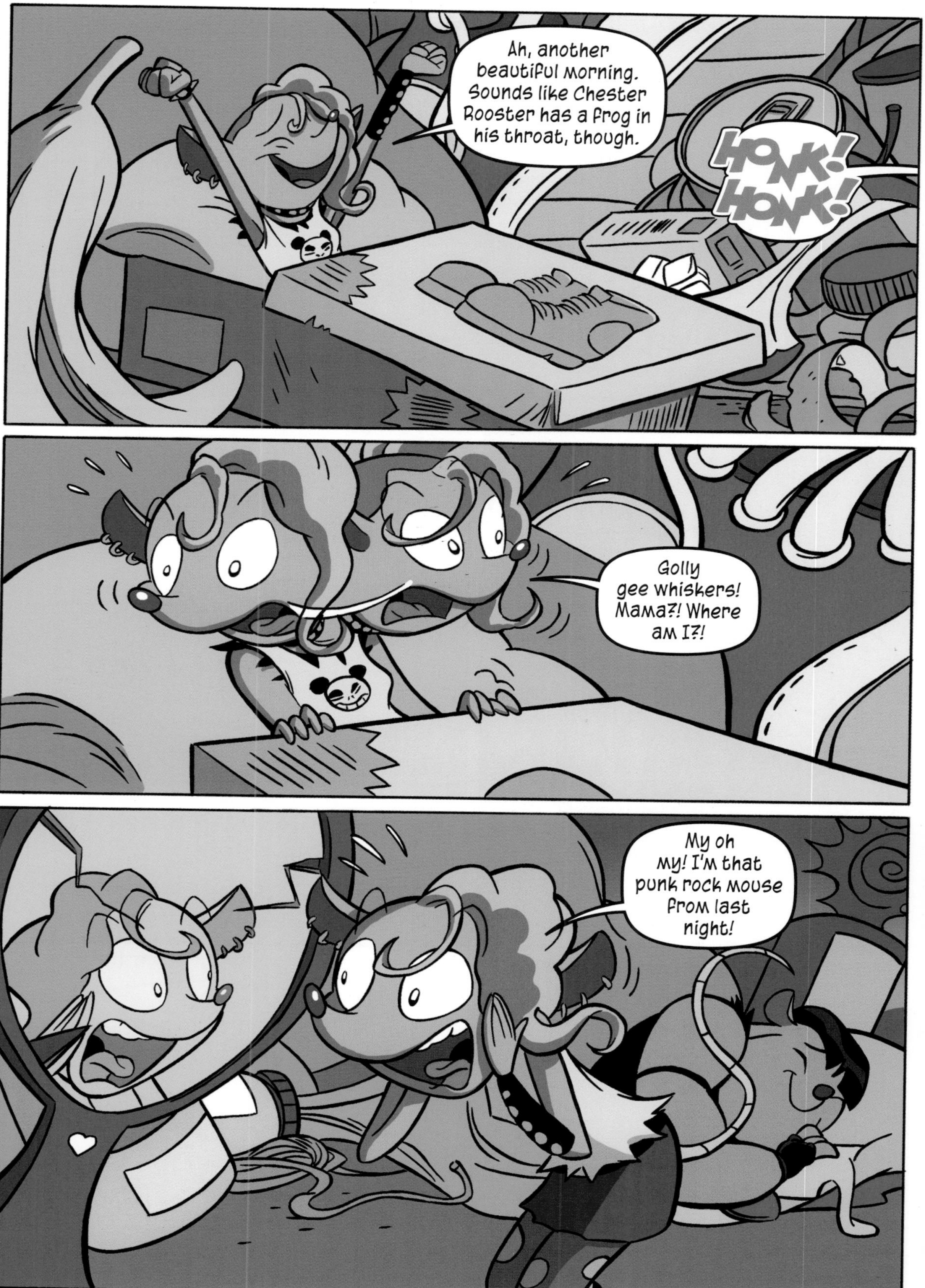
Ah, another beautiful morning. Sounds like Chester Rooster has a frog in his throat, though.
HONK! HONK!
Golly gee whiskers! Mama?! Where am I?!
My oh my! I'm that punk rock mouse from last night!

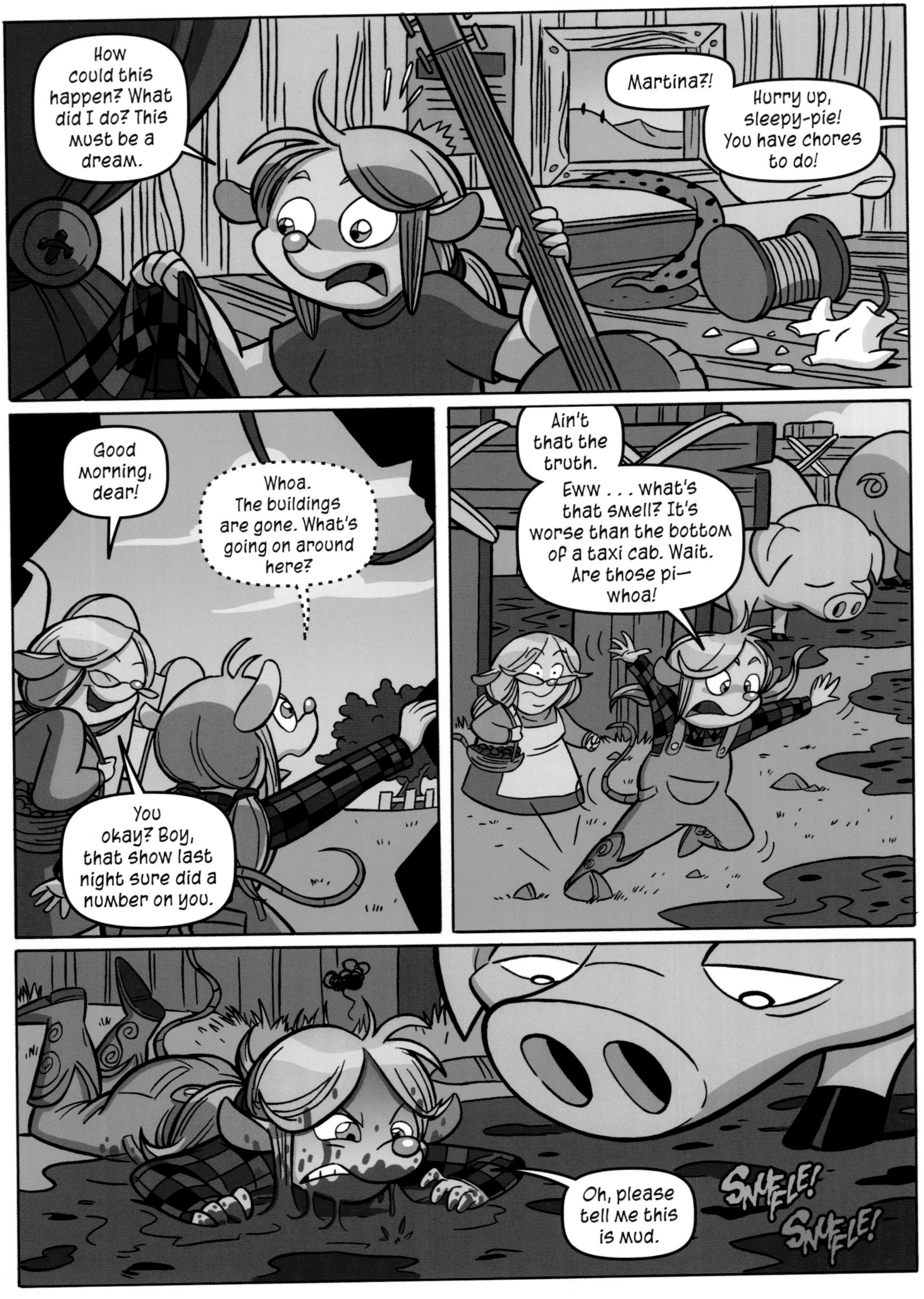
How could this happen? What did I do? This must be a dream.
Martina?!
Hurry up, sleepy-pie! You have chores to do!
Good Morning, dear!
Whoa. The buildings are gone. What's going on around here?
You okay? Boy, that show last night sure did a number on you.
Ain't that the truth.
Eww . . . what's that smell? It's worse than the bottom of a taxi cab. Wait. Are those pi— whoa!
Oh, please tell me this is mud.
SNUFFLE! SNUFFLE!

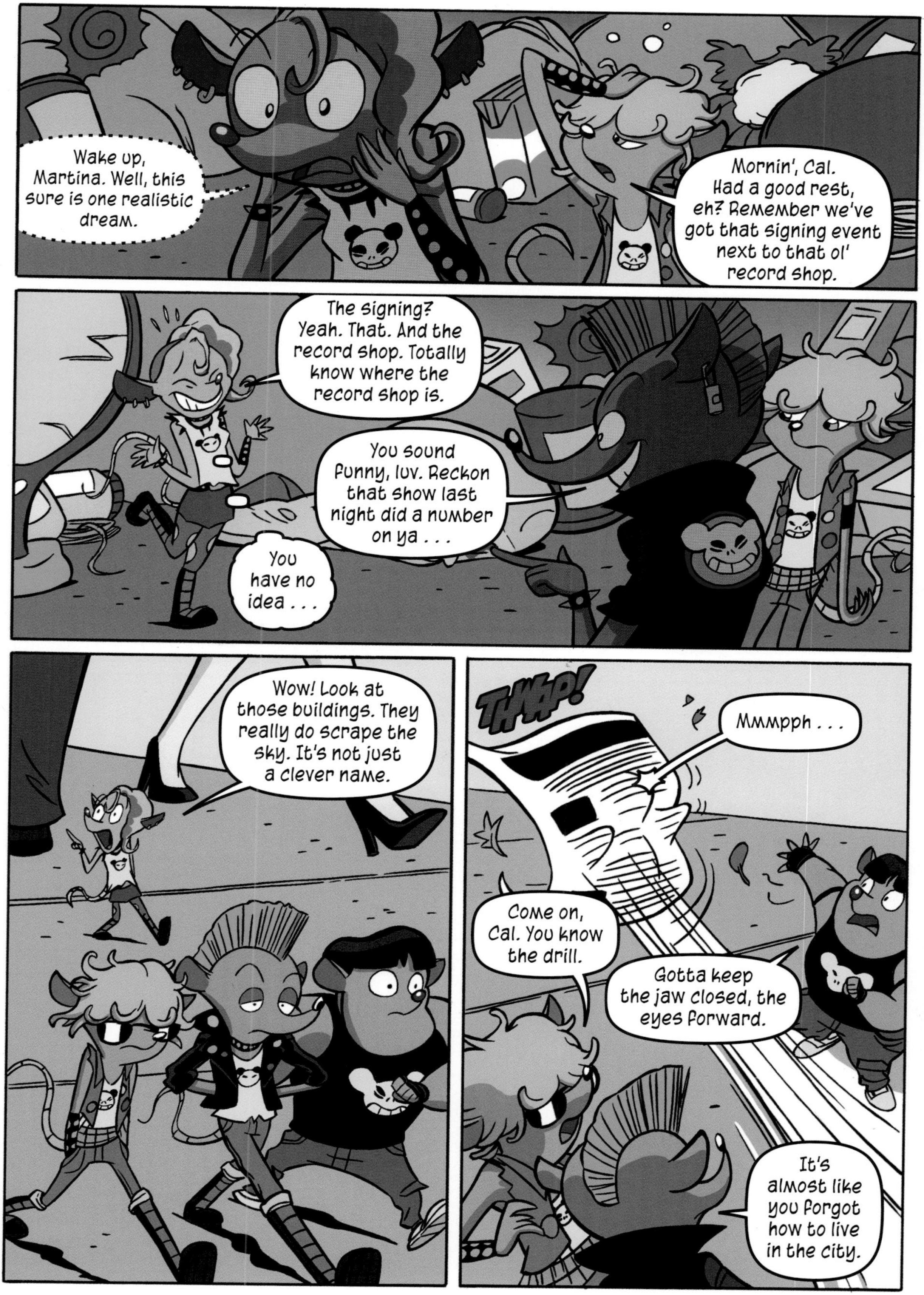
Wake up, Martina. Well, this sure is one realistic dream.
Mornin', Cal. Had a good rest, eh? Remember we've got that signing event next to that ol' record shop.
The signing? Yeah. That. And the record shop. Totally know where the record shop is.
You sound funny, luv. Reckon that show last night did a number on ya . . .
You have no idea . . .
Wow! Look at those buildings. They really do scrape the sky. It's not just a clever name.
THWAP!
Mmmpph . . .
Come on, Cal. You know the drill.
Gotta keep the jaw closed, the eyes forward.
It's almost like you forgot how to live in the city.

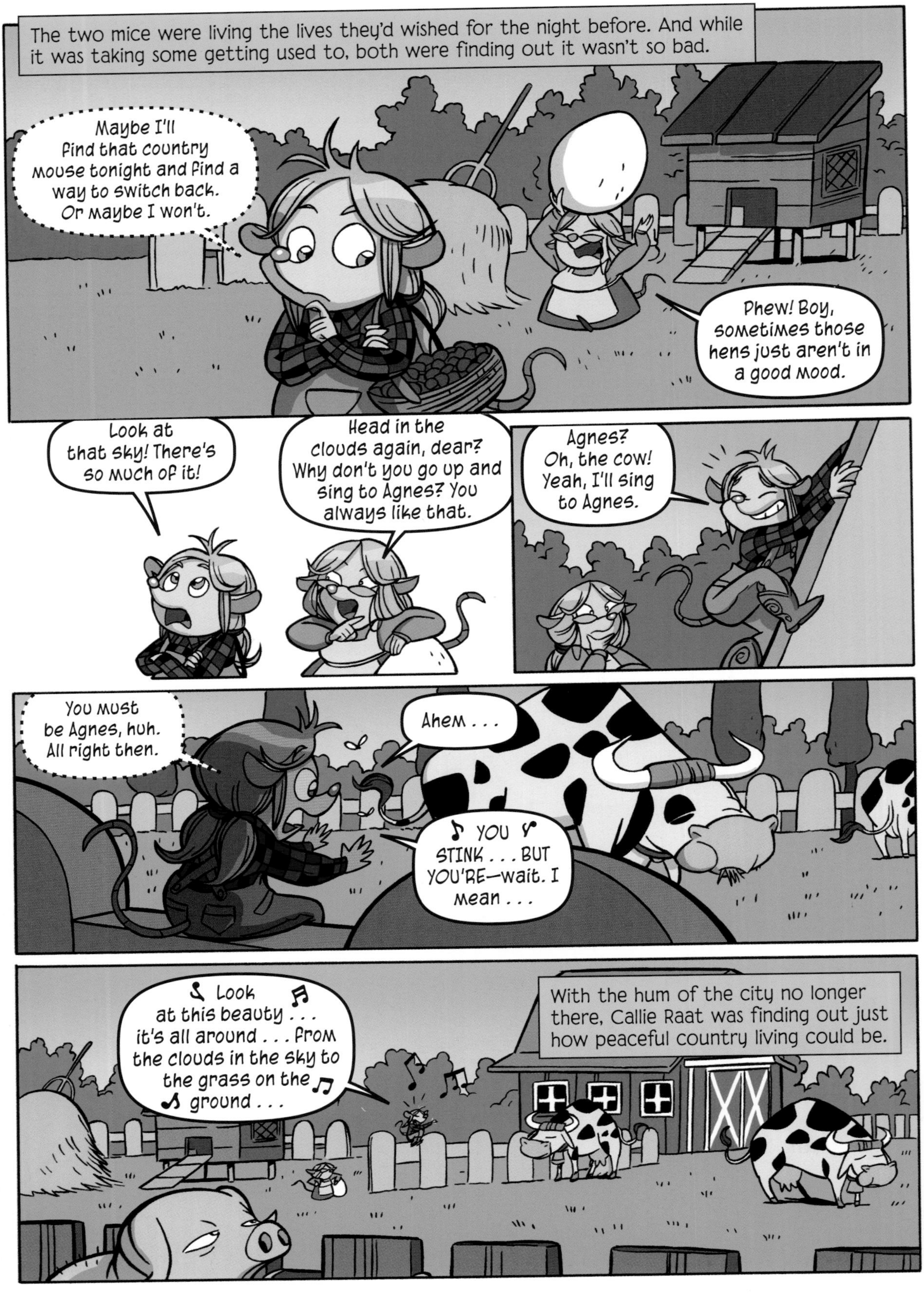
The two mice were living the lives they'd wished for the night before. And while it was taking some getting used to, both were finding out it wasn't so bad.
Maybe I'll find that country mouse tonight and find a way to switch back. Or maybe I won't.
Phew! Boy, sometimes those hens just aren't in a good mood.
Look at that sky! There's so much of it!
Head in the clouds again, dear? Why don't you go up and sing to Agnes? You always like that.
Agnes? Oh, the cow! Yeah, I'll sing to Agnes.
You must be Agnes, huh. All right then.
Ahem . . .
YOU STINK . . . BUT YOU'RE—wait. I mean . . .
Look at this beauty . . . it's all around . . . from the clouds in the sky to the grass on the ground . . .
With the hum of the city no longer there, Callie Raat was finding out just how peaceful country living could be.

Meanwhile, in the city . . .

COMIC BOOKS

FINAL VYNIL RECORDS & MORE

ONE WAY

ONE WAY

STOP

HONK! HONK!

Hey! Watch it!

MICE-Fits! I'm your biggest fan!

No, I am! Sign my album!

Patience! You'll all get paw-tographs!

ARCADE MICE

rat punk

MOUSE N' ROSES
THE HAVARTI INCIDENT

Oh my goodness. It's really you.

Yep. That's me. Um . . . Callie Raat.

I love you!

MICE FITS

They really love Callie. Huh. I could get used to this.

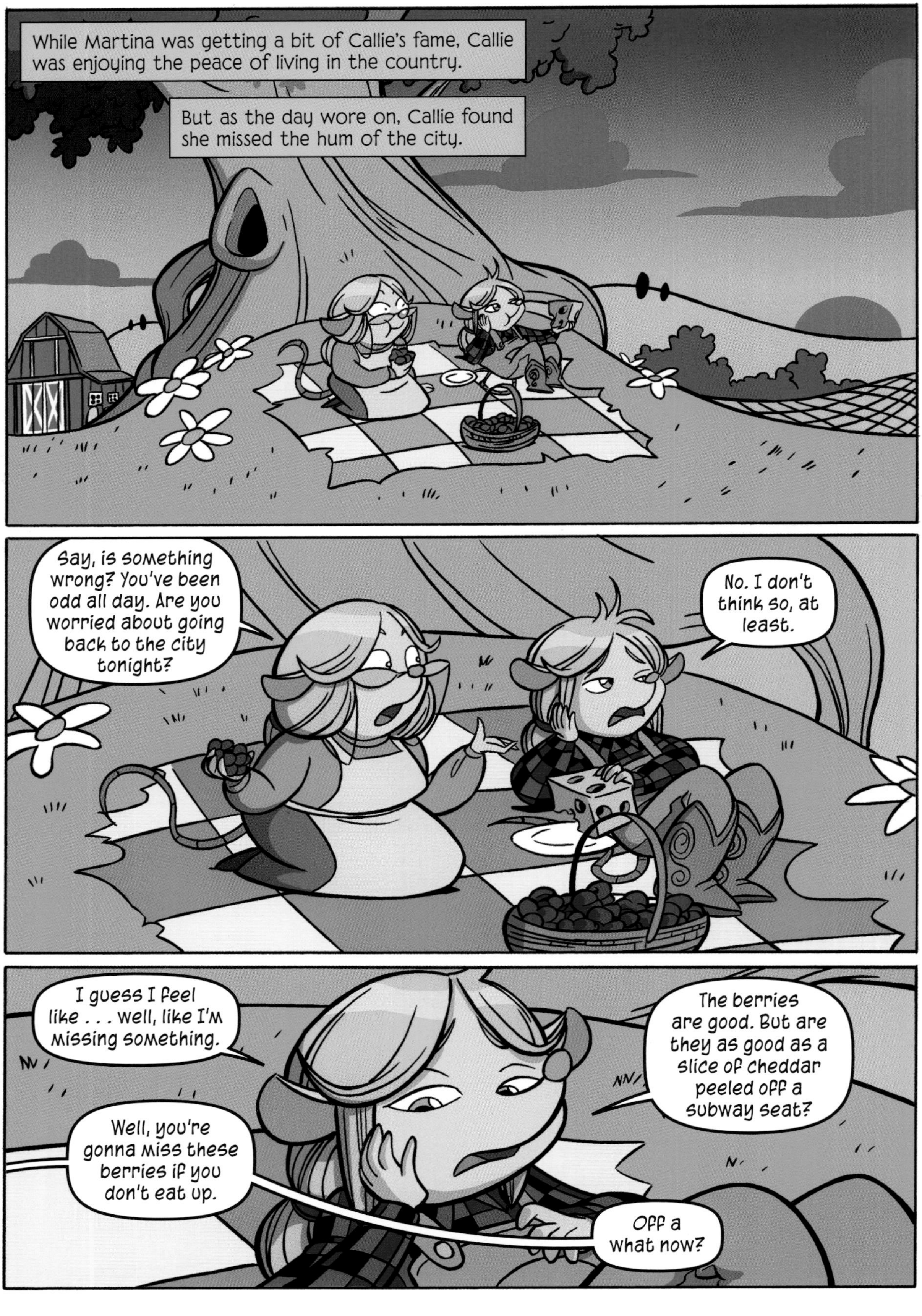
While Martina was getting a bit of Callie's fame, Callie was enjoying the peace of living in the country.
But as the day wore on, Callie found she missed the hum of the city.
Say, is something wrong? You've been odd all day. Are you worried about going back to the city tonight?
No. I don't think so, at least.
I guess I feel like . . . well, like I'm missing something.
Well, you're gonna miss these berries if you don't eat up.
The berries are good. But are they as good as a slice of cheddar peeled off a subway seat?
Off a what now?

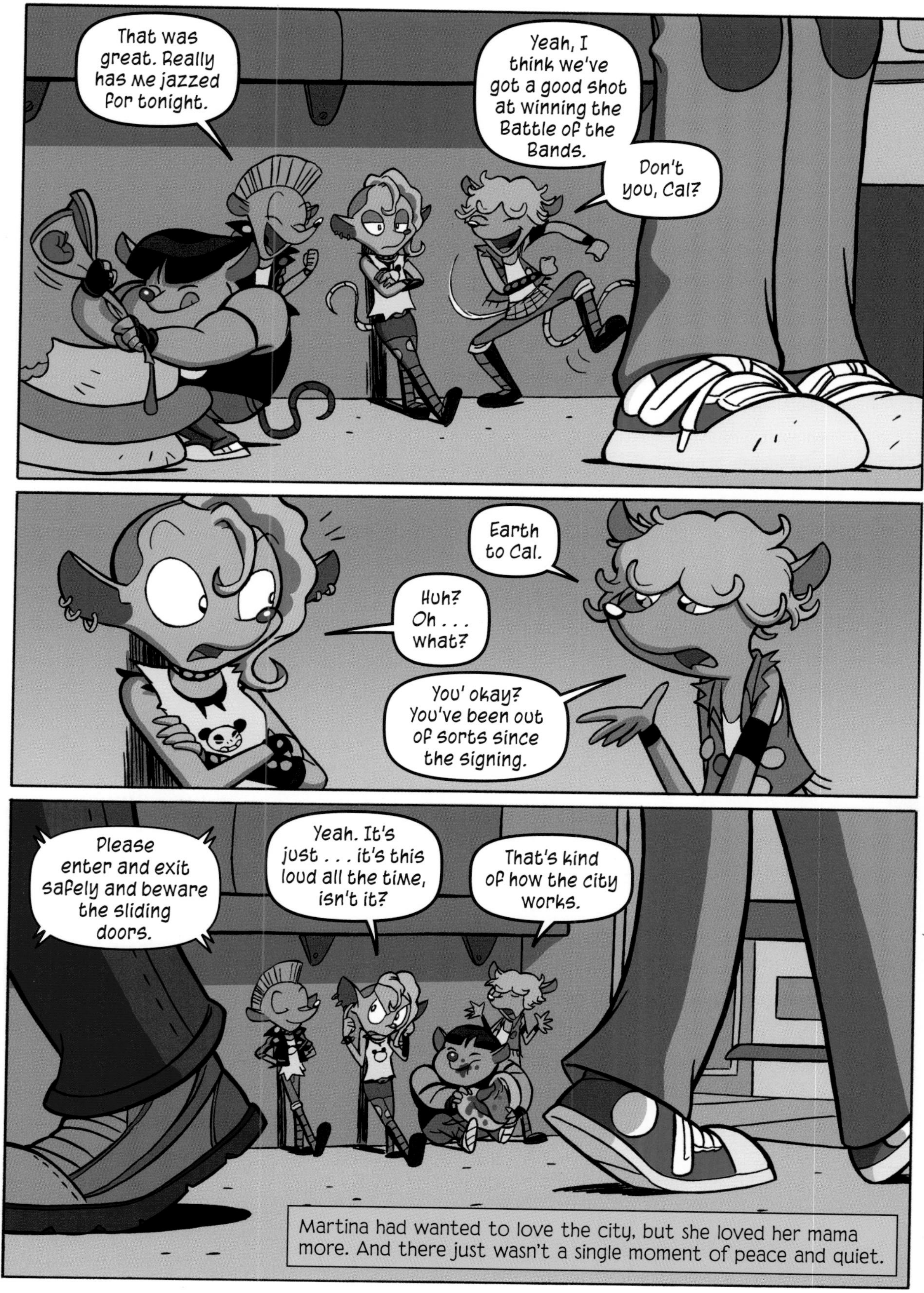
That was great. Really has me jazzed for tonight.
Yeah, I think we've got a good shot at winning the Battle of the Bands.
Don't you, Cal?
Earth to Cal.
Huh? Oh . . . what?
You' okay? You've been out of sorts since the signing.
Please enter and exit safely and beware the sliding doors.
Yeah. It's just . . . it's this loud all the time, isn't it?
That's kind of how the city works.
Martina had wanted to love the city, but she loved her mama more. And there just wasn't a single moment of peace and quiet.

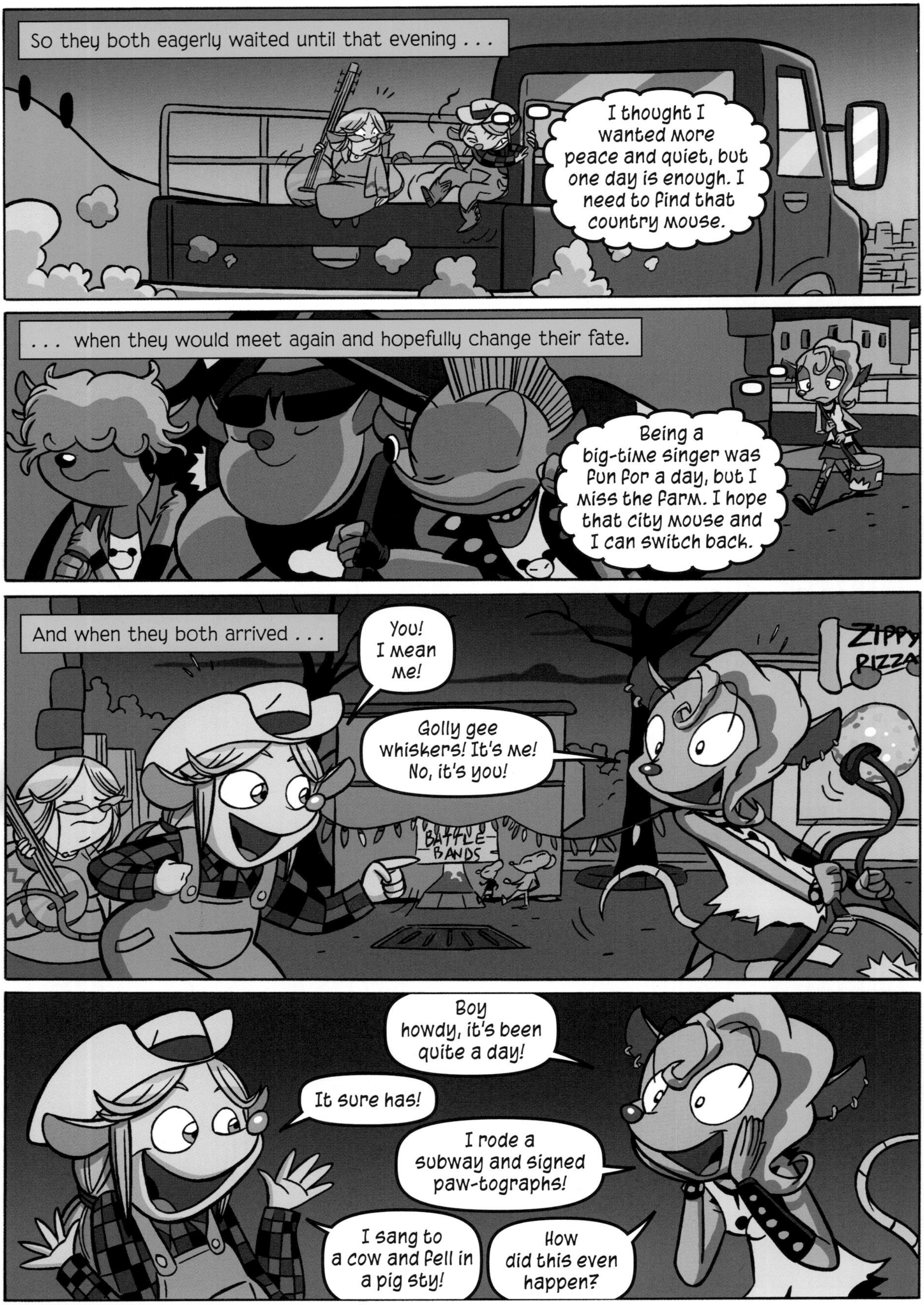
So they both eagerly waited until that evening . . .
I thought I wanted more peace and quiet, but one day is enough. I need to find that country mouse.
. . . when they would meet again and hopefully change their fate.
Being a big-time singer was fun for a day, but I miss the farm. I hope that city mouse and I can switch back.
And when they both arrived . . .
You! I mean me!
Golly gee whiskers! It's me! No, it's you!
ZIPPY PIZZA
BATTLE
BANDS
Boy howdy, it's been quite a day!
It sure has!
I rode a subway and signed paw-tographs!
I sang to a cow and fell in a pig sty!
How did this even happen?

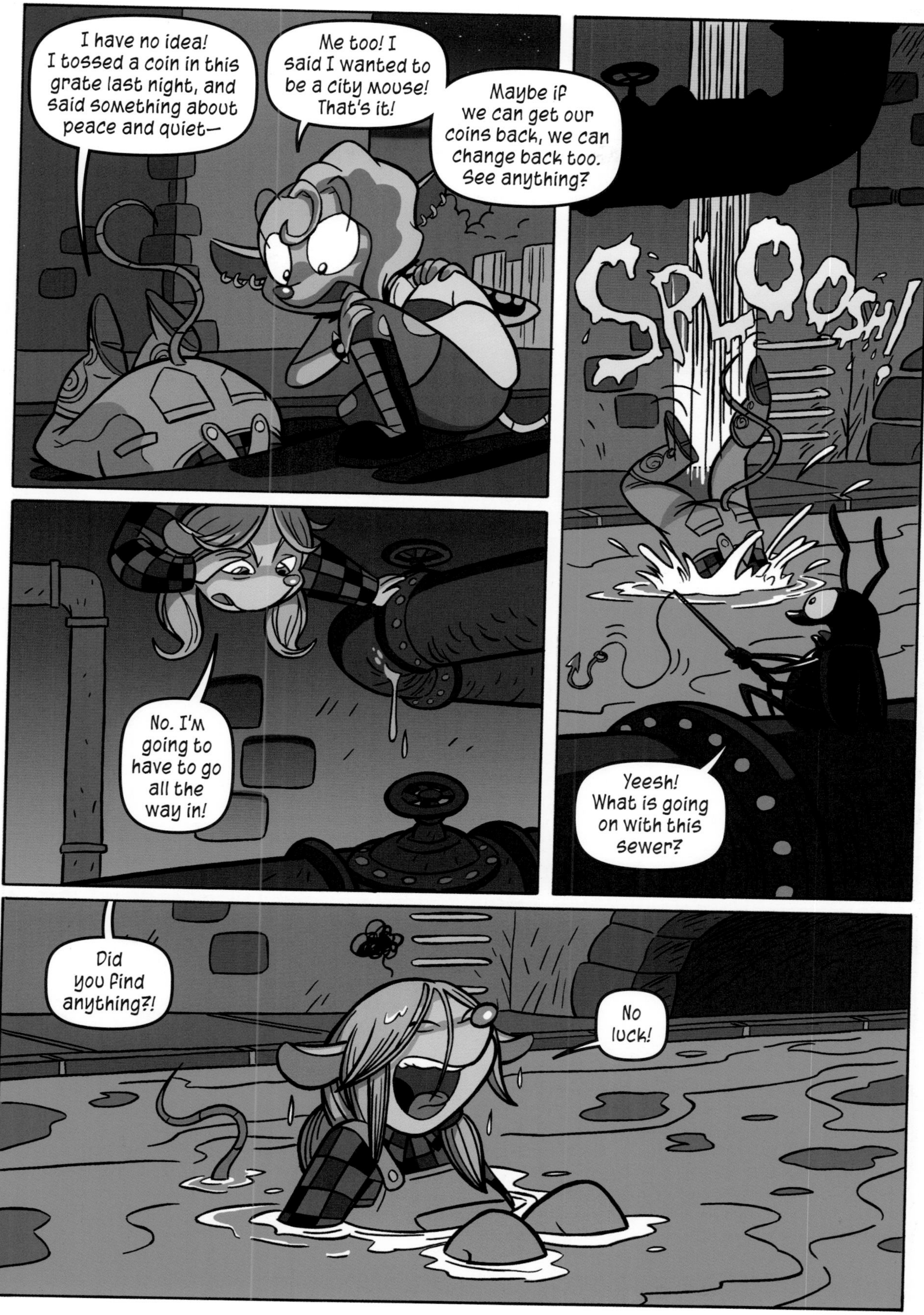
I have no idea! I tossed a coin in this grate last night, and said something about peace and quiet—
Me too! I said I wanted to be a city mouse! That's it!
Maybe if we can get our coins back, we can change back too. See anything?
SPLOOSH!
No. I'm going to have to go all the way in!
Yeesh! What is going on with this sewer?
Did you find anything?!
No luck!

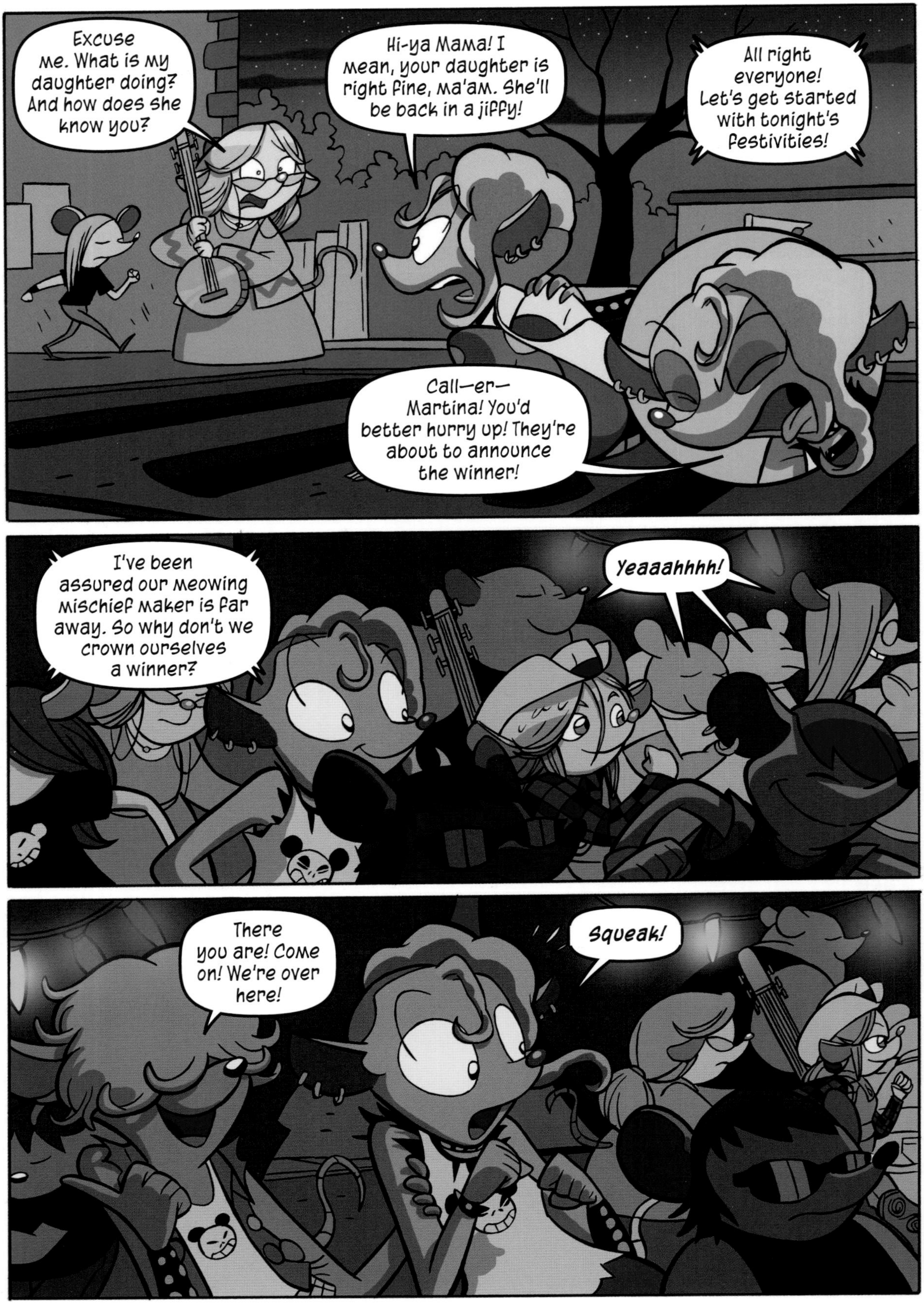

Excuse me. What is my daughter doing? And how does she know you?
Hi-ya Mama! I mean, your daughter is right fine, ma'am. She'll be back in a jiffy!
All right everyone! Let's get started with tonight's festivities!
Call—er—Martina! You'd better hurry up! They're about to announce the winner!
I've been assured our meowing mischief maker is far away. So why don't we crown ourselves a winner?
Yeaaahhhh!
There you are! Come on! We're over here!
Squeak!

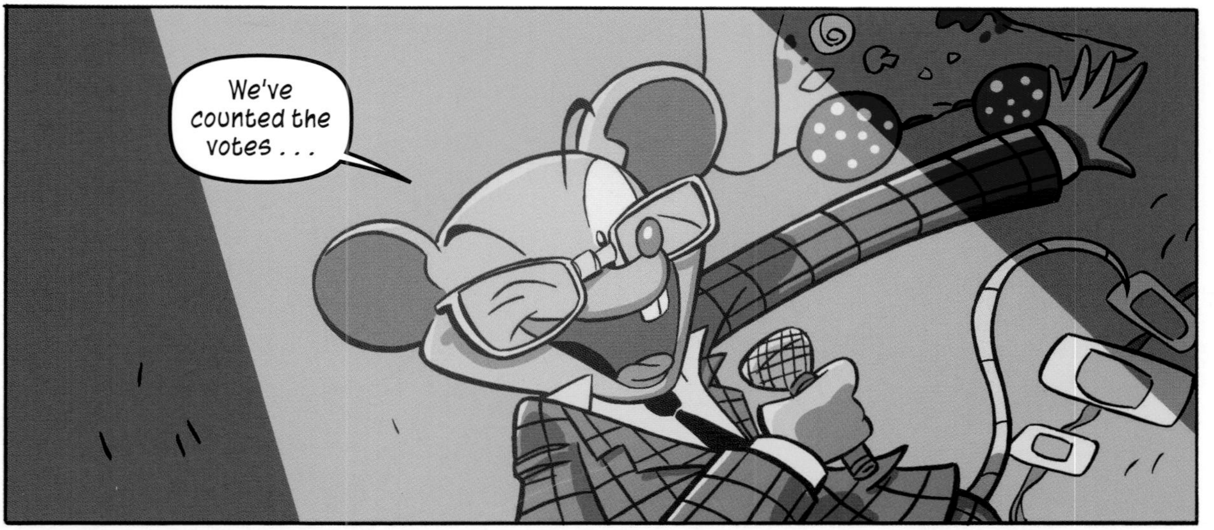
We've counted the votes . . .

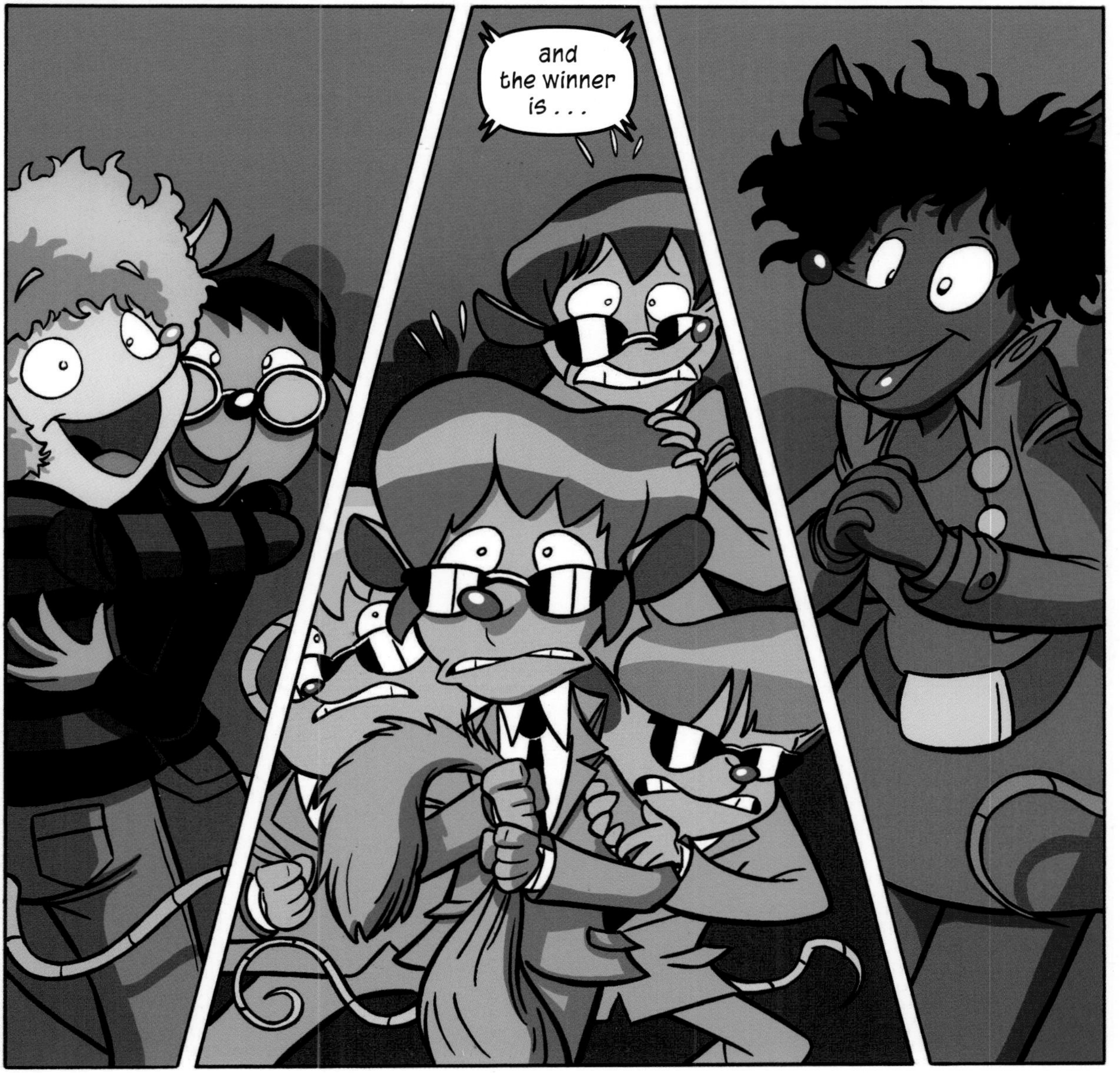
and the winner is . . .

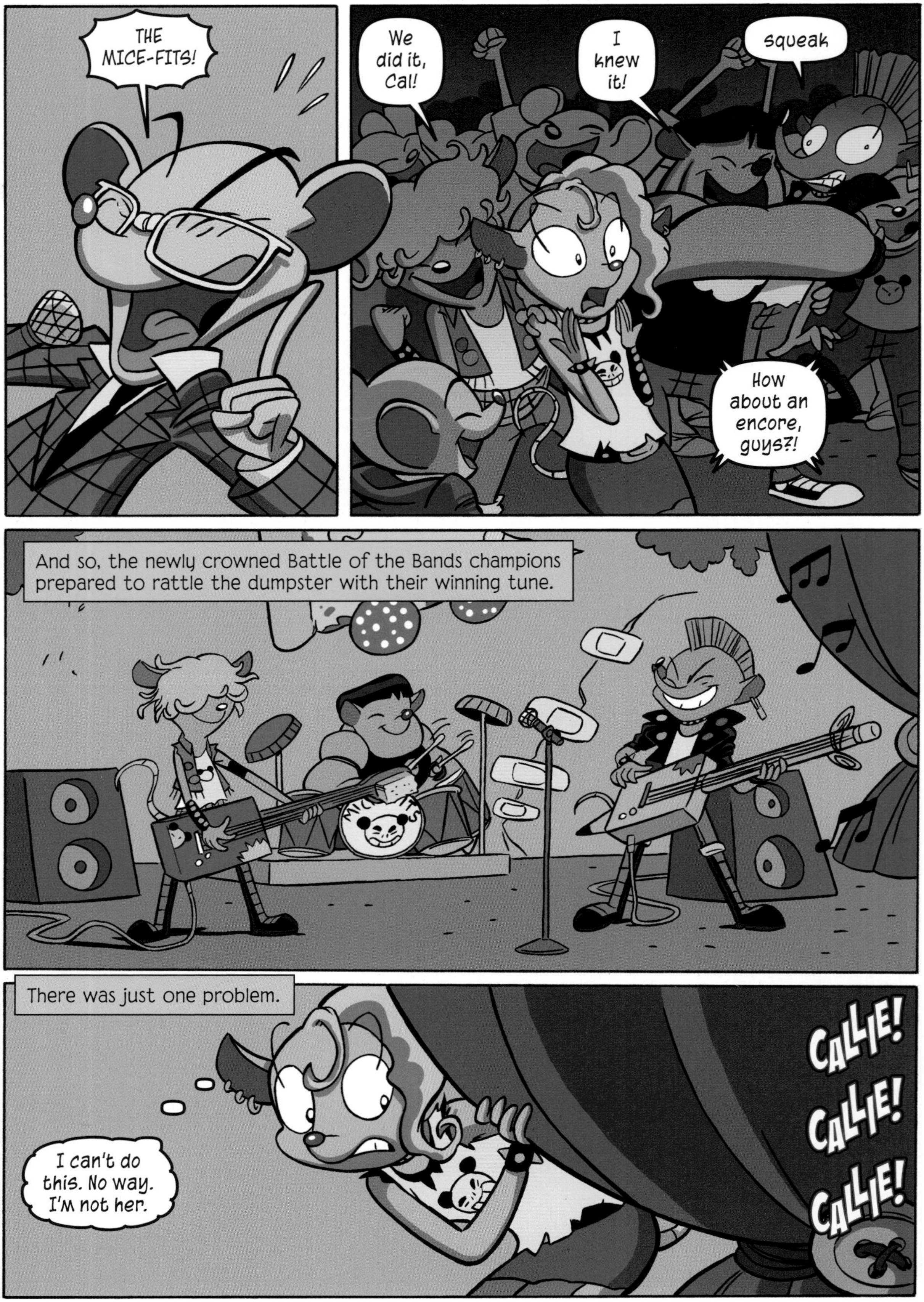
THE MICE-FITS!
We did it, Cal!
I knew it!
squeak
How about an encore, guys?!
And so, the newly crowned Battle of the Bands champions prepared to rattle the dumpster with their winning tune.
There was just one problem.
I can't do this. No way. I'm not her.
CALLIE!
CALLIE!
CALLIE!

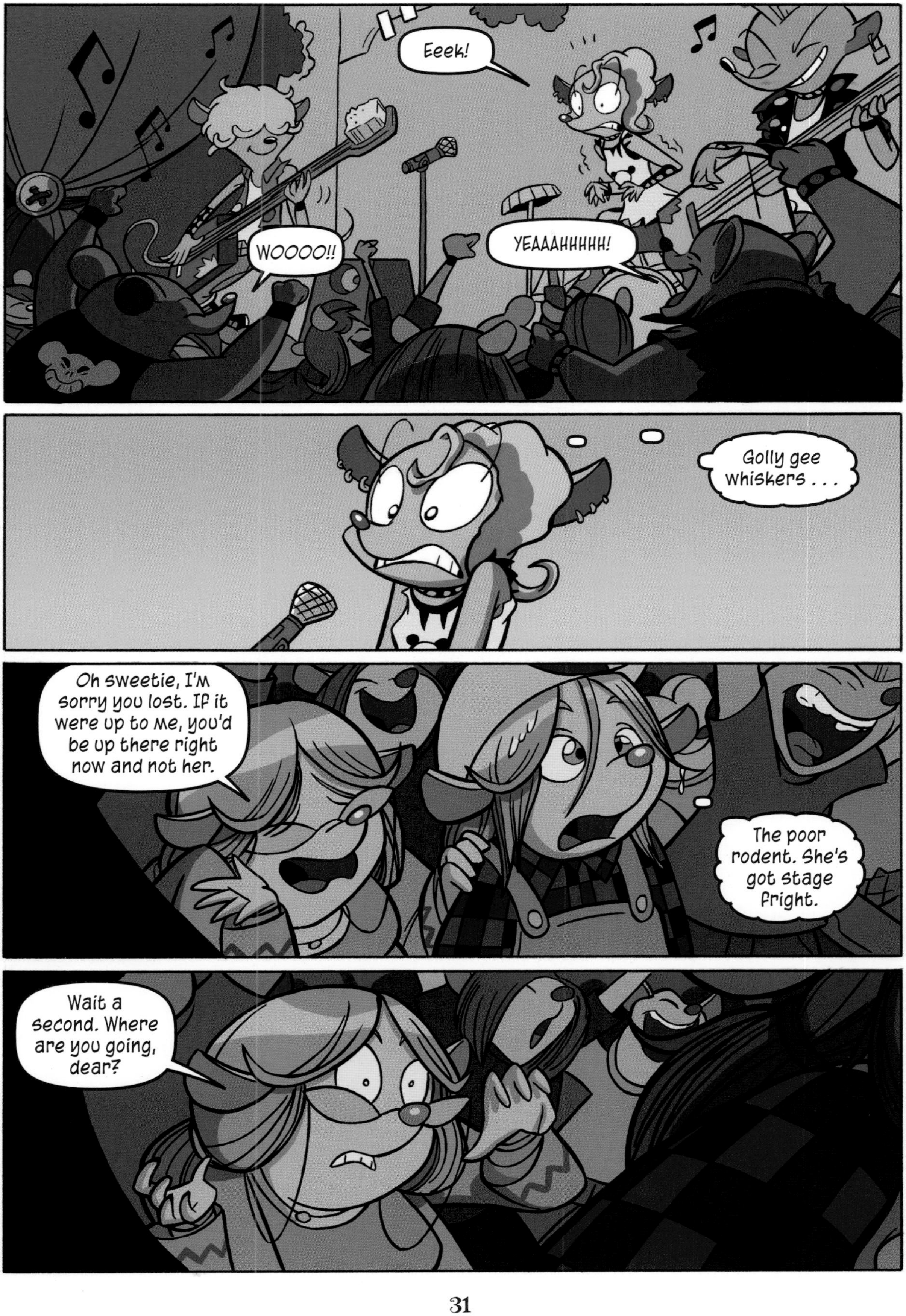
Eeek!
WOOOO!!
YEAAAHHHHH!
Golly gee whiskers . . .
Oh sweetie, I'm sorry you lost. If it were up to me, you'd be up there right now and not her.
The poor rodent. She's got stage fright.
Wait a second. Where are you going, dear?

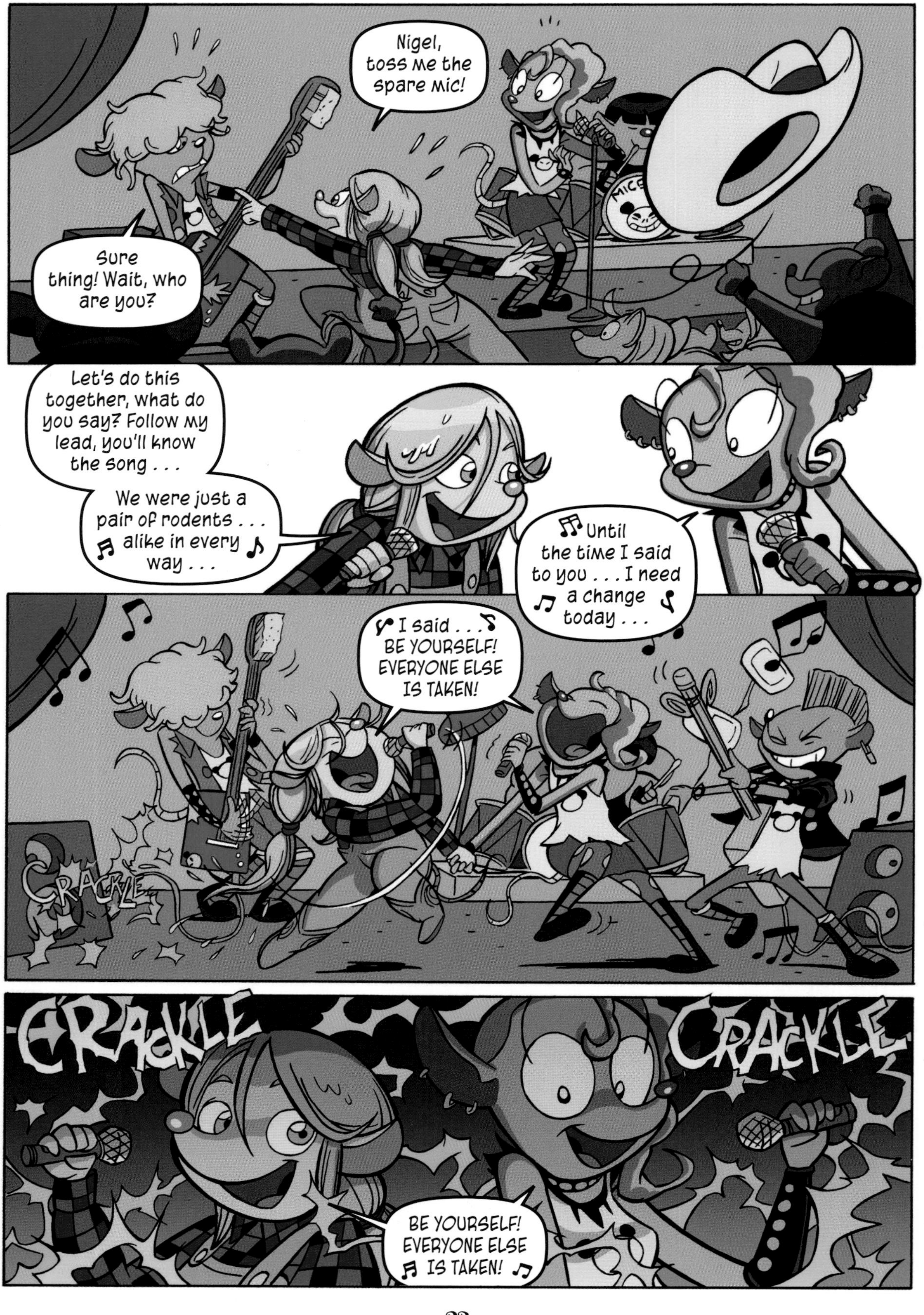
Nigel, toss me the spare mic!
Sure thing! Wait, who are you?
MICE
Let's do this together, what do you say? Follow my lead, you'll know the song . . .
We were just a pair of rodents . . . ♫ alike in every way . . .
♫ Until the time I said to you . . . I need ♫ a change today . . .
I said . . . BE YOURSELF! EVERYONE ELSE IS TAKEN!
CRACKLE
CRACKLE
CRACKLE
BE YOURSELF! EVERYONE ELSE ♫ IS TAKEN! ♫

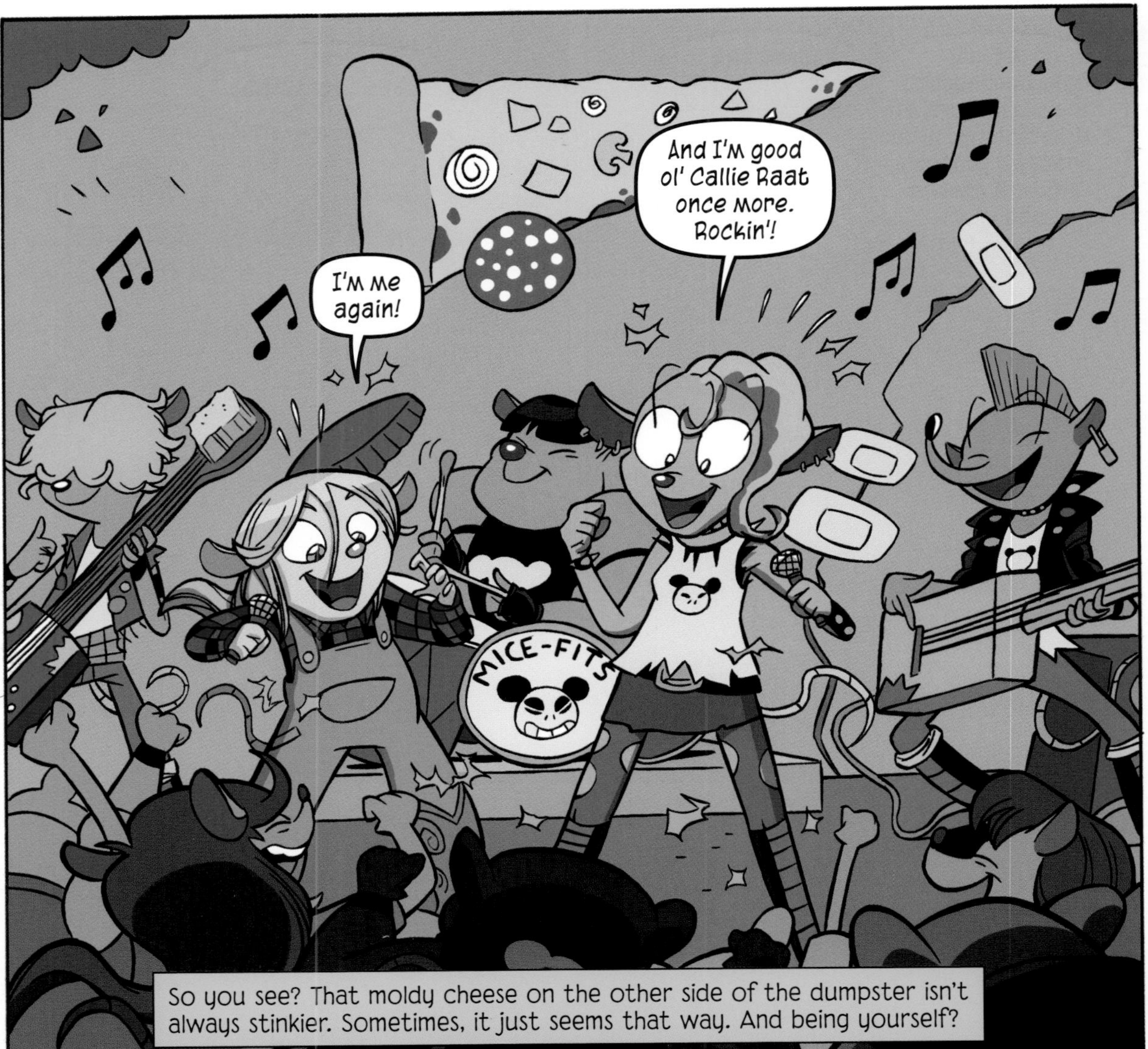
I'm me again!
And I'm good ol' Callie Raat once more. Rockin'!
MICE-FITS
So you see? That moldy cheese on the other side of the dumpster isn't always stinkier. Sometimes, it just seems that way. And being yourself?

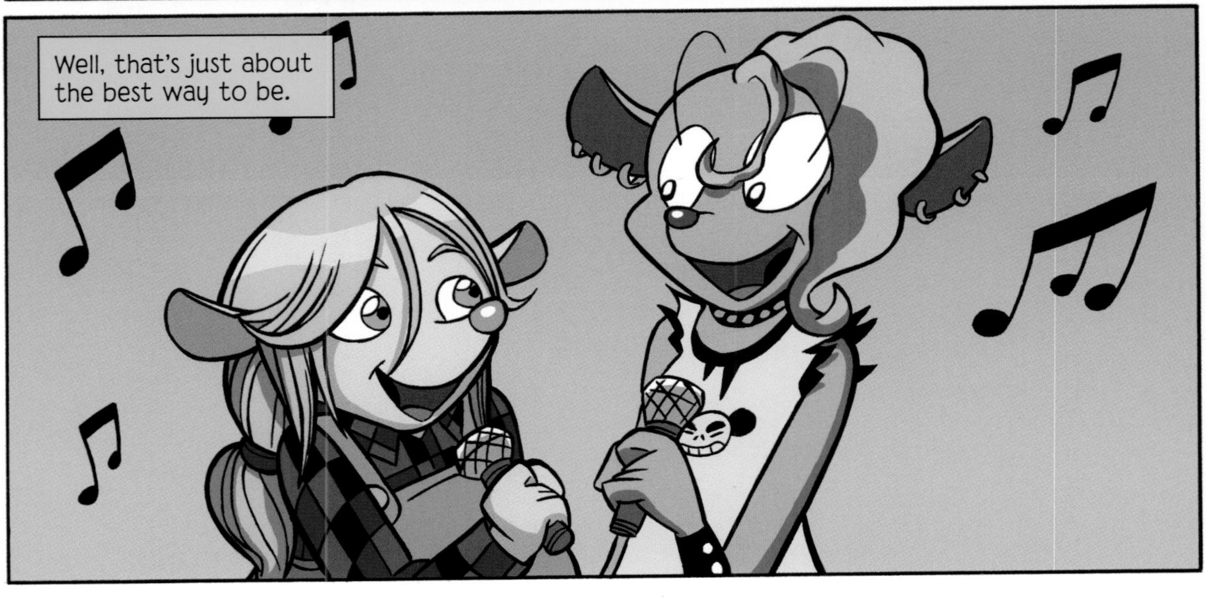
Well, that's just about the best way to be.

ALL ABOUT FABLES

A fable is a short tale that teaches the reader a lesson about life, often with animal characters. Most fables were first told thousands of years ago by a Greek storyteller named Aesop. At the end of a fable, there's almost always a moral (a fancy word for lesson) stated right out so you don't miss it. Yes, fables can be kind of bossy, but they usually give pretty good advice. Read on to learn more about Aesop's original fable and its moral. Can you spot any other lessons?

THE TOWN MOUSE AND THE COUNTRY MOUSE

In the original fable, Town Mouse visits his cousin in the country. Country Mouse welcomes him with a meal of beans, bacon, cheese, and bread. This is meager compared to what Town Mouse is used to. He invites Country Mouse to the city to eat all kinds of delicious food.

In the city, Town Mouse offers his cousin food from a grand dining hall. There is more food than Country Mouse has ever seen! However, as they eat, a pair of large dogs race into the hall, frightening the poor Country Mouse. He scampers away, back to the country.

THE MORAL

Better to live simply in safety than living the high life in fear. (In other words, no food is worth dogs chasing you!)

A FAR OUT GUIDE TO THE FABLE'S MAGICAL TWISTS!

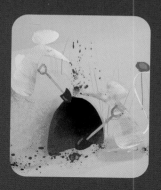

In Aesop's fable, the town mouse and country mouse are cousins. Here, they are strangers.

The fable has the town mouse visiting the mouse that lives in the country. The two mice do not switch bodies!

Dogs, and not a stray cat, are what frightens the mice in the original tail . . . I mean tale.

In the original fable, the moral is that living simply in safety is better than living in high style in fear. In the new twist, the moral is to be happy with who you are.

VISUAL QUESTIONS

Is the character speaking or singing in this panel? How can you tell?

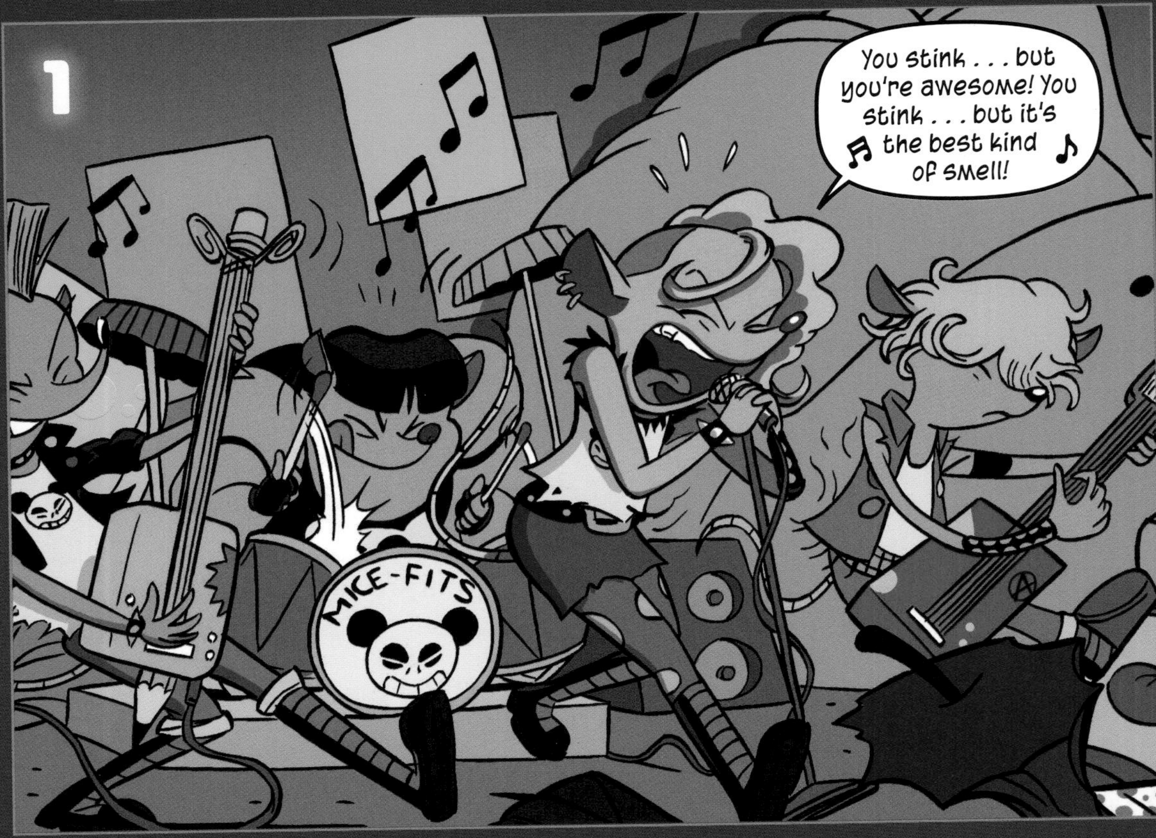
1
You stink . . . but you're awesome! You stink . . . but it's the best kind of smell!
MICE-FITS

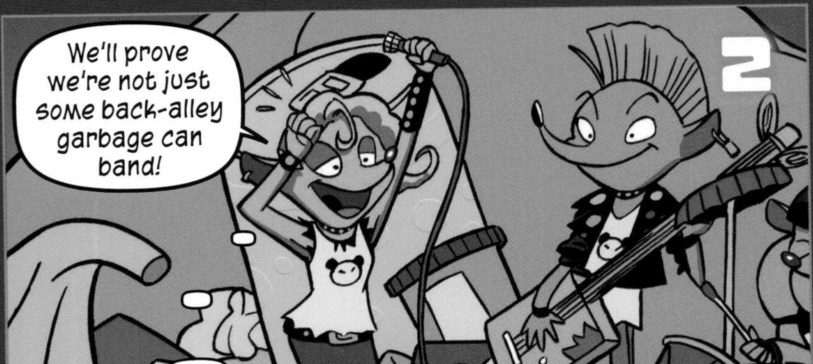
2
We'll prove we're not just some back-alley garbage can band!
Boy, I'm beat. I wonder what it'd be like away from the pressure to perform. To just . . . be a singer.
MICE-FITS

Callie Raat's speech is positive and upbeat here, but her thought bubble shows that she's really exhausted. Do you see any other clues to show how tired she is?

These panels are set up to show two things happening at the same time. What do you think is happening here? What clues tell you this?

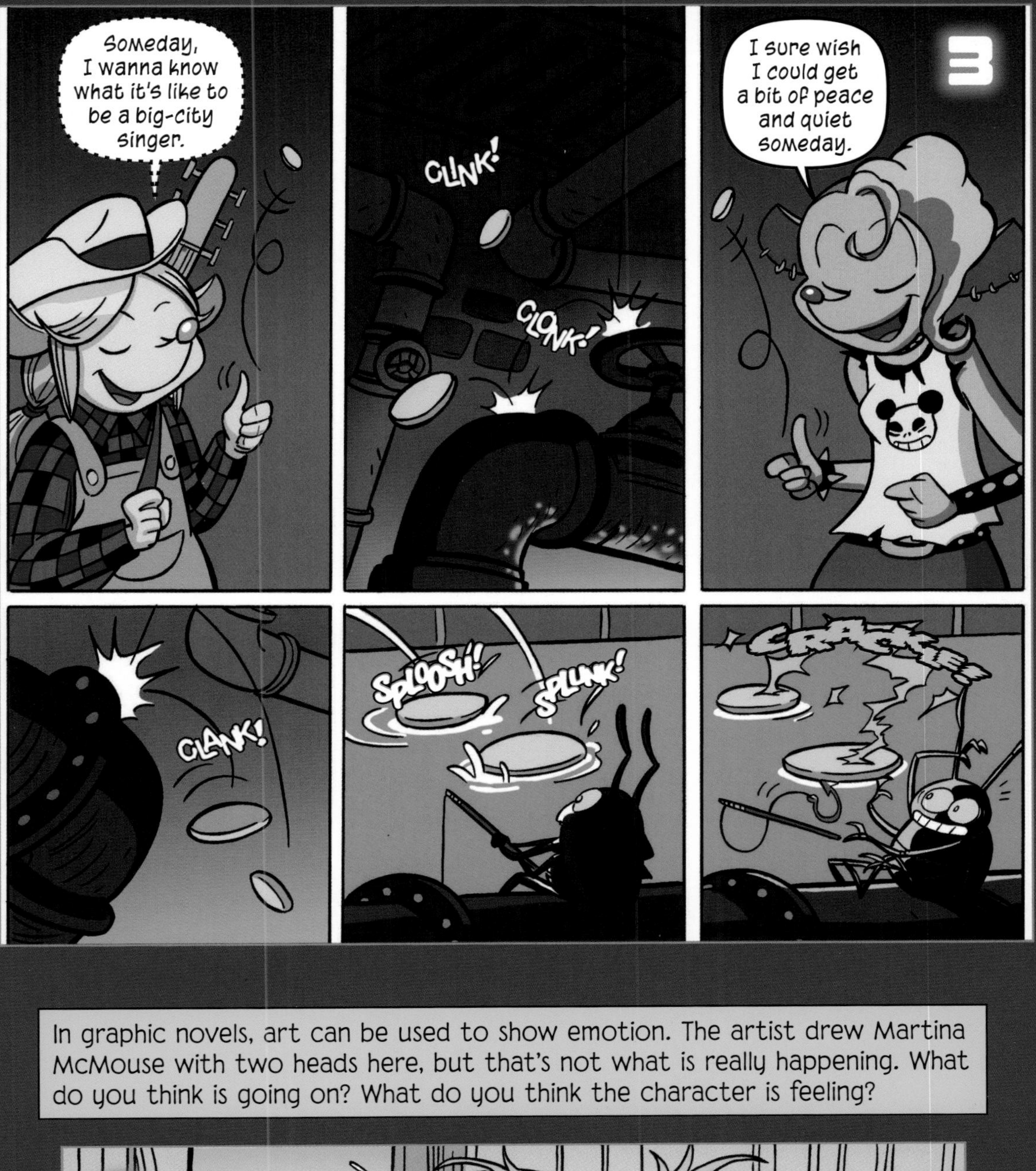
3
Someday, I wanna know what it's like to be a big-city singer.
CLINK!
CLONK!
I sure wish I could get a bit of peace and quiet someday.
CLANK!
SPLOOSH!
SPLUNK!
CRACKLE

In graphic novels, art can be used to show emotion. The artist drew Martina McMouse with two heads here, but that's not what is really happening. What do you think is going on? What do you think the character is feeling?

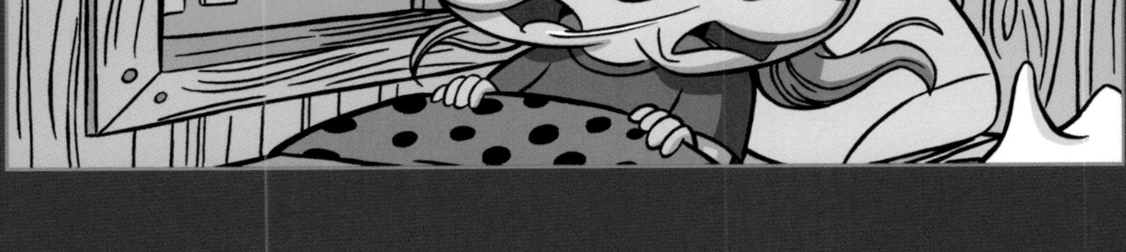
4

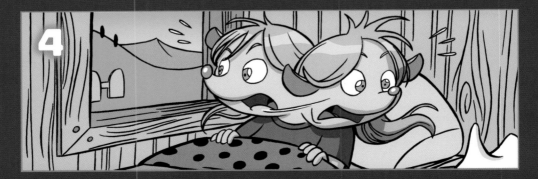

AUTHOR

Brandon Terrell is the author of nearly 100 books, ranging from action-packed sports stories and graphic novels to spooky tales and mind-boggling mysteries. He is a graduate of Hamline University's Master of Fine Arts in Writing for Children and Young Adults program. When not hunched over his laptop writing, Brandon enjoys watching movies and television, reading, cooking, and spending time with his wife and two children in Minnesota.

ILLUSTRATOR

Alex Lopez is from Sabadell, Spain. He became a professional illustrator and comic book artist in 2001, but he has been drawing ever since he can remember. Lopez's pieces have been published in many countries, including the United States, United Kingdom, Spain, France, Italy, Belgium, and Turkey. He's also worked on a variety of projects, from illustrated books to video games to marketing pieces . . . but what he loves most is making comic books.

GLOSSARY

chorus (KOR-uhs)—the part of a song that is repeated after each verse

contestant (kuhn-TES-tuhnt)—someone competing in a contest, such as a rocking battle of the bands

encore (AHN-kor)—a song played after a band ends the main part of a concert

fable (FAY-buhl)—a short tale to teach a moral lesson, often with animals as characters

feast (FEEST)—a large, fancy meal for a lot of people on a special occasion

meager (MEE-gur)—very little, or barely enough

menacing (MEN-uh-SING)—describes something that threatens to cause evil, harm, or injury

paw-tograph (PAW-toe-graf)—a famous animal's handwritten name—at least the name of an animal with paws

rodent (ROHD-uhnt)—a mammal with long front teeth used for gnawing; rats, mice, and squirrels are rodents

sewer (SOO-ur)—a system, often an underground pipe, that carries away liquid and solid waste

THE MORAL OF THE STORY IS... EPIC!

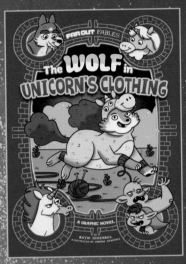

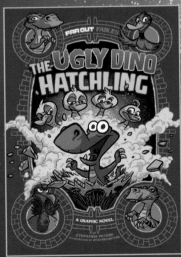

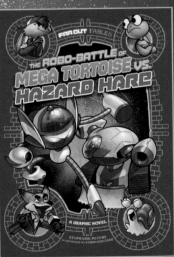

FAR OUT FABLES